T0329263

Old Christmas

Kathryn Brocato

Crimson Romance

New York London Toronto Sydney New Delhi

CRIMSON
ROMANCE

Crimson Romance
An Imprint of Simon & Schuster, Inc.
1230 Avenue of the Americas
New York, NY 10020

For information about special discounts for bulk purchases, please contact Simon & Schuster Special Sales at 1-866-506-1949 or business@simonandschuster.com.

The Simon & Schuster Speakers Bureau can bring authors to your live event. For more information or to book an event contact the Simon & Schuster Speakers Bureau at 1-866-248-3049 or visit our website at www.simonspeakers.com.

ISBN: 978-1-4405-5164-2
ISBN: 978-1-4405-5144-4 (ebook)

Dedication

THIS BOOK IS DEDICATED TO

MY HUSBAND,

CHARLES S. BROCATO

"THE MAN FROM BEAUMONT"

WHOSE PRIZE-WINNING RECIPE FOR

"DEEP DARK SECRET CHEESECAKE"

IS INCLUDED AT THE END OF THE BOOK

Chapter 1

Casey Gray stood on the doorstep until she'd gotten her emotions under control. When the door opened, she glanced around the Johnsons' big living room, viewing the cacophony of chatter, Christmas music, cheerful lights, and people inside as if through a dark portal.

Outside, the cool, humid darkness of a Southeast Texas winter night beckoned with a promise of starlight and solitude—and the postponement of a potentially humiliating confrontation.

"Come on in, Casey. I'm so glad I ran into you today." Merrick Johnson, a former classmate, pulled her inside. "Look who's back in town, folks. Our famous local chef, Casey Gray."

Merrick's azure-blue eyes and overdone friendliness hadn't changed a bit, Casey observed, but her red-blond hair had been lightened to a silvery color, her makeup imitated a natural tan, and the slinky, black pajama-like outfit she wore enhanced both.

An image of another pair of blue eyes the color of a cloudless winter sky, framed by thick, black brows and long, straight lashes filled Casey's mind. The eyes smiled into hers, loving and eager. She made herself call up an image of those eyes as she had last seen them—narrowed, contemptuous, and angry.

Casey smiled and nodded toward the few curious faces that turned her way. "Thank you for inviting me," she said to Merrick.

"Are you kidding? And turn down the chance to have a genuine French-trained chef cook for the crowd? I'd have to be crazy. The kitchen's all yours."

Casey smiled. She was well aware that Merrick had invited her tonight for a purpose, so she'd made her plans in advance. She had once spent many happy hours cooking in the Johnson kitchen, and had used that fact to hint that Merrick's guests might enjoy a special, freshly baked treat. Merrick had leaped on the suggestion.

An enormous Christmas tree dominated one corner of the living room, designer-decorated with wooden country-style ornaments and red bows. Piles of gifts wrapped in green, red, and silver lay stacked beneath it.

Casey pretended to admire the tree while using the toe of her shoe to open any cards she could reach for the one name she was interested in. When she found it, her heart contracted with an emotion that might have been pain or joy, or both.

"I had no idea you were in town. Why didn't you call me?" Bonnie Brite, a short brunette who had long been Casey's best friend, rushed over to fling both arms around her.

"When I got in, I went straight to the hospital and ran into Merrick." Casey tossed back her shoulder-length chestnut hair and smiled. "She said you'd be here tonight."

"How is your grandmother? As soon as I heard she was sick, I hoped you'd come home." Bonnie stepped back and stared at her.

"She's better, I think. I'm waiting to see Dr. Johnson in the morning."

"God, don't you look fantastic," Bonnie said. "Love that crinkly hairdo on you. And look at the little wool business suit. It's too hot, even in winter." Bonnie grabbed Casey's arm. "Let's go in the kitchen where it's quieter. I'm dying to hear all about your job in New York."

Casey, who wanted to forget about her job in New York, said quickly, "I'm dying to hear all about the beauty shop. Believe me, it's a lot more interesting."

"Hah. You know what it's like around here. The biggest event of the year is the Rice Festival, and I didn't even go this year. But I'll tell you who did. Old Kalin McBryde was there, checking out the Rice Cooking Contest. If you want to know what I think—"

"I don't." Casey softened the words with a smile.

"—he's still crazy about you," Bonnie finished, unabashed.

Casey followed Bonnie past several people she didn't know despite having grown up in the small Southeast Texas town of Winnie.

Strange, how she'd heard of Kalin McBryde all her life, thanks to Merrick's bragging, but had never met him until he spotted her struggling to get her Rice Cooking Contest entries inside the Community Building her junior year in high school.

"I don't see anyone here I know," Casey observed.

"Is that so surprising? No one can kill a party, even her own, faster than Merrick. Do you know what they say about her at law school?"

Casey could imagine it. "No."

"They claim she'll single-handedly close down the Texas Bar Association with all her talk about her future greatness. You know. She's going to be a great lawyer like her uncle, Walter McBryde, the great criminal attorney. She leaves Kalin out of her spiel now, for which I'm sure he's grateful."

"Merrick's okay," Casey said, grinning.

Casey banished memories of Kalin chasing her through this very room and catching her in the kitchen. "Dr. and Mrs. Johnson must have left the house to Merrick for the weekend. Look at that." She pointed to the trays bearing an assortment of cheeses, chips, pickles, nuts, and sandwiches laid out on the dining room table. She added in tones of loathing, "Party trays. Sheer laziness on Merrick's part. She ought to be ashamed."

"Spoken like a true professional. Can you really run a big restaurant by yourself, cooking and all?"

"You bet. The first thing I'd do in here is pitch out all that garbage." Casey led the way into the modern white kitchen. "Look at this wonderful equipment. Mrs. Johnson is a great cook, and Merrick never learned a thing from her."

"Merrick believes her brain is too good for anything domestic." Bonnie dissolved into laughter. "And you're right. Those trays are still full."

Casey opened the refrigerator and peered inside. "Look at that. Full of milk and eggs. The possibilities are endless."

"I can't believe you." Bonnie's short, black curls quivered with mock outrage. "The living room is full of sexy young law students, and you'd rather be back here in the kitchen making something for everyone to eat. You haven't changed a bit." Her glare morphed into a grin. "I'm so glad you're back."

"The only person I really hoped to see tonight was you. Stick around. I'm about to bless this gathering with something far more interesting than that excuse for party food in the dining room." Casey straightened and smiled at her friend.

Merrick entered with a good-looking, red-headed man. "Look who's back, Clay. Casey Gray. Say, Casey, you never graduated from college, did you? What a shame. Dad always said you had a good mind."

Casey said, with enormous calm, "I graduated from International Culinary College in Baltimore, which was exactly what I had planned to do all my life."

"It's a shame so many people think you're ignorant unless you've been to college," Merrick observed.

Bonnie, who had become a licensed cosmetologist rather than a bachelor of arts or sciences, pressed her lips together and cast her gaze to the ceiling. The red-headed man glanced from Merrick to Casey with mild curiosity.

Merrick added, "I wouldn't have missed the college experience for anything."

"I've decided you're right, Merrick. I think I'll sign up for law school tomorrow," Casey said, straight-faced.

Merrick's azure eyes, so like those of her cousin Kalin, went impossibly wide. "You want to go to law school? Do you have any idea what you're talking about?"

Casey looked at her hopefully. "I'm counting on you to set me straight. I figured that if I apply this week . . . "

Merrick, looking horrified, proceeded to set her straight, detailing a process that required about five years, upright ancestors all the way back to the American Revolution, and a mind like Einstein's. Casey pretended great interest.

"Anyway, if you still want to go to law school," Merrick finished, "I'll be happy to show you what courses to take in college to prepare yourself."

"I'd appreciate that, Merrick. It sounds like a lot of work, but I'm sure it'll be worthwhile."

"It's the best thing that ever happened to me," Merrick said, in all earnest. She glanced at the large yellow kitchen clock. "Are you sure you have time to bake something?"

"After culinary school I spent six months in Paris training under some of the top chefs. I'm fast. It'll only take an hour."

"Have at it," Merrick invited. "Mom always said you were wonderful in the kitchen."

Casey wasted no time in shedding her jacket and rolling up the sleeves of her creamy silk blouse. She tied on one of the voluminous aprons hanging on a hook beside the door and ignored Merrick and her male friend.

The red-headed man, Clay, took a sudden interest. "You're a cook?" He studied Casey from the top of her chestnut head to the tips of her high-heeled pumps. "You don't look like any cook I ever saw before. Are you as good as Julia Child?"

Casey smiled from the depths of a cabinet. "Wait and see."

Clay took his cell phone from his pocket and tapped on it. Casey hid a shudder and tried not to think of her own cell phone, lying dead in a charity collection bin in New York. She hated that phone. It symbolized everything she disliked about the city.

Clay looked up from the tiny screen and stared at Casey with the expression of a man who has come across a strange new specimen of womanhood and assessed her thick, wavy hair, large gray eyes, and slender, small-boned figure one more time.

"You're for real. You managed Chargois in New York."

"You're going to stay in here?" Merrick asked him and shot Casey a warning glance. "All right. I'll be right back."

Casey ignored the pair and opened each cabinet in turn, then studied the contents of the freezer. She abstracted a box of frozen puff pastry and laid it on the cabinet to defrost.

"You aren't going to be any fun for the rest of the night," Bonnie complained. "Aren't you even going to use a recipe?"

"If I were you," Casey said, from deep within the recesses of a tall cabinet, "I'd go visit in the living room for a while. I'm going to be busy for the next hour or so."

"I'd rather visit with you." Bonnie sat down at the table.

Casey came out of the cabinet clutching a box of cake flour. "I'm about to produce something that will be worth the wait."

"You're going to bake a cake?" Clay regarded the cake flour with awe as Casey seized a measuring cup and poured out exactly two cups of flour.

"I'm going to bake a *gateau*." Casey set a pan of water on the stove and turned on the gas. "I don't think anyone here has ever eaten a French *gateau*."

Bonnie stared. "Well, I'll be."

Clay's green eyes followed Casey. "Ah. Now I know who you are. You used to date Kalin McBryde, didn't you?" His tone let Casey know Merrick had been talking.

"That was back when Bonnie and Merrick and I were in high school." She smiled and measured sugar, then stood on the tips of her toes to reach a copper bowl hanging on the wall, which she took to the sink and cleaned carefully with salt and vinegar. "Are you in law school with Merrick?"

Clay declined to answer.

Merrick entered the kitchen and ran a red-tipped hand through her silvery hair. Upon seeing Casey cracking eggs into the copper bowl under the interested gaze of her current flame, she said, "What's up, gang?"

"We were determining who was in law school with you." Casey poured in sugar, set the copper bowl over the pan of now-boiling water on the stove, and beat it energetically with a wire whisk.

"You're making a cake like that?" Merrick watched the operation, then seated herself beside Clay and sighed with overdone nostalgia. "I remember when my cousin Kalin used to take loaves of homemade bread Casey had baked back to school with him. Kalin is Walter McBryde's son. You know, the great criminal attorney." She looked at Bonnie.

"We know." Bonnie managed not to laugh.

"Casey, did you know Kalin just sold a book?" Merrick asked. "He told Dad last week. I didn't even know he wrote. Did you?"

"Casey used to read all his manuscripts," Bonnie said.

Merrick's eyes opened wide, and she looked with disbelief from Bonnie to Casey.

Casey's heart leaped with an emotion she tentatively identified as joy. She tested her batter by lifting the whisk and allowing a trail of batter to fall. "That's wonderful news, Merrick. I'm very happy for him."

She fought to blank out the image of Kalin, black brows drawn together in a straight bar, eyes blazing, clutching a thick stack of paper and arguing with her over whether or not his cowboy hero should have a girlfriend.

Clay glanced at his cell phone. "No wonder the poor guy can't make a go of his practice. He should have gone to work for one of the big law firms if he can't cut it on his own."

"I can't understand him." Merrick frowned. "With his name and connections, he could be as rich and powerful as his father."

Casey switched off the heat and transferred the copper bowl to the table, where she continued to whisk. "Kalin always said he couldn't defend a client he suspected was guilty."

She smiled at the memory of Kalin getting into trouble when he refused to lie about running his Viper over a flowerbed.

"Cheez," Clay said beneath his breath.

"Most of us have to remind ourselves that in our legal system, each person is entitled to the best representation," Merrick hastened to explain.

"Kalin never wanted to go to law school in the first place," Casey said. An image of Kalin's hopeful, tanned face and bright blue eyes as he'd told her his plans for writing several Western novels a year overlaid the thick foam she was whisking.

Merrick stood, thinning her reddened lips angrily. Her chair scraped the floor as she shoved it back. "That's ridiculous, Casey Gray. The truth is, you were holding him back. It's a good thing he realized that before it was too late."

Merrick, Casey remembered, truly believed law school was the culmination of a worthy upbringing, reserved for the select few with the money and connections to get in. The attitude had reaped a lot of good-natured mockery for Merrick in high school.

Casey sifted flour over the thick foam in the copper bowl and folded it in, French-style, with her fingers, well aware that Merrick felt personally attacked. She poured the batter into a springform pan she had sitting ready with a steady hand.

"In that case, it doesn't matter, does it?" she said. "Kalin went to law school and can now rise as far as his ability takes him." She popped the pan into the oven she had preheated, then cleaned her fingers without concern.

Placated, Merrick returned to her chair. "I don't know what's gotten into him. He simply refuses to work at it. What did you do to him?"

"What did I do to him?" Casey repeated, amused. "I haven't seen Kalin in five years, so if he isn't progressing as you think he ought, it's by his own choice." She gathered up bowls and the whisk and carried them to the sink. Poor Kalin. Why was he practicing law when he disliked almost everything having to do with it?

She'd known this party would be difficult. Busying herself with familiar tasks in the kitchen helped, but with Merrick discussing Kalin, not even the kitchen was a haven.

"I've always wondered, Casey," Merrick said, after sitting a moment in thoughtful silence. "We thought you weren't leaving for culinary school until the fall, but instead, you left the summer you graduated from high school. Did you leave early because Kalin broke up with you?"

Despite a lifetime of knowing Merrick's tendency to tread in areas angels avoided, Casey hadn't expected anything this nosy. She saw only one way to stop the discussion. "Of course." She smiled and rinsed out the copper bowl. "I thought it would be better all the way around if I left early. That way, Kalin wouldn't have to run into me every time he came to Winnie to go fishing or hunting with your dad."

Merrick went speechless for once as she belatedly sensed her audience's discomfiture.

"Wise move." Clay stared at Casey after according Merrick one bored glance. "Obviously, McBryde is hopeless."

Casey measured eggs, milk, and sugar into a pan with great outward calm and applied the wire whisk to the mixture.

"That was very thoughtful of you, Casey." Merrick's face glowed bright red.

Casey bit her lip and maintained a straight face. To the accompaniment of dead silence, she took a wooden spoon from a drawer, transferred the pan to the stove, and stirred.

"By the way, Merrick." Casey took pity on the blond. "Did you make it to the Rice Festival? Who won the cooking contest?"

"Heavens, I have no idea." Merrick looked relieved. "I was busy in school, so I didn't come home, but I did hear Teddy Buckley won the Rice Eating Contest. Isn't that about like him?"

Casey, pleased with the success of her diversion, kept stirring while Merrick and Bonnie exchanged reasonably friendly comments on Teddy Buckley.

Merrick looked up suddenly. "You know, Casey, it's really amazing how little you resemble your father."

At that, Bonnie prepared to wade into Merrick, and Casey gave her a warning glance. "I hope I don't resemble him at all."

It was hard to tell whether Merrick was trying to deliberately humiliate Casey, or whether she was being her usual tactless self. Casey reflected with inward laughter that it was a good thing she had prepared herself to deal with Merrick's habit of dredging up one's darkest secrets for discussion. Merrick's boyfriend, Clay, was likely to transfer to another law school very soon, judging from his expression.

"Well, why on earth not?" Merrick leaned forward. "He was so handsome, besides being a movie star. Unless, of course, he wasn't your father. Did you ever contact him before he died?"

"I was too young then." Casey's tone reflected major disinterest. She bent to peer in the oven window at her cake.

Bonnie took the cue. "How's the cake, Casey? Are you sure you didn't leave something out? Like the baking powder?"

Casey smiled. "This cake won't need any."

"Her father was a movie star?" Clay let his eyes wander appreciatively over what could be seen of Casey beneath the big apron. "I believe it."

"Derrick Davenport." Merrick looked proud to be the one revealing this tidbit. "Casey's mother, if you can believe it, went to Hollywood when she was about eighteen to become an actress. Instead, she wound up pregnant and publicly begging Derrick to marry her. He got out of it, which always made me wonder. Did he leave you anything in his will, Casey?"

Clay stared at Casey's profile. "She must have been very beautiful."

Casey remained unmoved. "No, he didn't leave me a thing, which is just as well. I wouldn't have taken it."

Merrick clearly found this hard to believe. "Do you think he really was your father, or was your mother just making it up?"

"I don't know," Casey said in non-encouraging tones. "He never had anything to do with me, nor I with him. So far as I'm concerned, both my parents died at my birth."

"That's a healthy attitude," Merrick said. "If I thought my father was Derrick Davenport, I'd be telling the world. I couldn't believe it when

I found out you had never told Kalin, as close as you two had been."

Casey shrugged. "Since a court of law had determined Mr. Davenport innocent of fathering me, in spite of the DNA evidence, what good would it have done to claim otherwise?"

"She has his eyes," Clay said suddenly.

The group stared at Casey's face, and Casey was hard-put to keep stirring without reddening. She had long ago realized that she did indeed possess Derrick Davenport's distinctive, sparkling gray eyes framed with the same dark, curly lashes. That discovery, however, instead of making her proud, had shamed her.

"Casey's right," Bonnie said quickly. "What good does it do at this late date?"

Clay nodded and fingered his phone, still staring at Casey.

Merrick looked at him. "Kalin always talked about how beautiful Casey's eyes were. He was furious when he learned who her father was. *Allegedly* was, that is."

Casey removed her pan from the heat, extracted her cake from the oven, and flipped it expertly upside down onto a cooling rack.

"McBryde was always weird," Clay pronounced.

Casey glanced up and smiled.

"Well, you can't blame him," Merrick said, in the judicious tones of one who has thought things over very carefully. "When he broke up with her, Casey made a public scene begging him not to leave her. What else could he think but that she was doing the same act her mother had? At that time, the McBrydes were wealthy, you know." She added, "Of course, anyone who has known Casey as long as I have knows that she's not the type to try and shame Kalin into marrying her. But it was embarrassing, all the same."

Casey adjusted the oven temperature and unrolled a sheet of puff pastry onto a piece of waxed paper. As she worked it over with a rolling pin, a vision of the last time she'd seen Kalin McBryde arose in her mind. She had been practically on her knees, begging him just to listen to her.

Even the bare memory was a knife-like thrust to the heart. But she had known that scene would be mentioned tonight. She had performed about one thousand creative visualization exercises in order to be able to deal with it. She could handle it.

Bonnie sat up straighter and glared at Merrick. "Don't you think you ought to change the subject? After all, it's none of our business in the least."

Casey turned away to search the cabinets quickly and returned with a package of dried beans. She fitted a piece of tin foil into the pastry, filled it with dried beans and ran it into the oven. Concentrating on every practiced movement helped her maintain her composure. By the time she returned to the table, Merrick sat in depressed silence while the other two enthusiastically discussed their plans for the upcoming Christmas holiday.

Casey fetched her cake from its cooling rack and picked up a long, thin knife. "Merrick, don't you usually go skiing over the holidays?" She removed the cake from its pan.

"Not this year." Merrick looked thankful. "I've got to study. If you do go to law school, you'll find out what I mean."

"I'm sure I will." Casey expertly sliced the single cake into three thin layers.

Clay stared. "You're really planning on going to law school?"

"You needn't sound so astonished," Casey said, tongue-in-cheek. "Merrick is one of the best salespeople a law school could have."

"I believe in what I'm doing." Merrick tossed back her silvery hair, seemingly unaware of the humor in Casey's voice. "Does Kalin know you're planning on going to law school, Casey?"

"You'll have to be sure to mention it to him."

"I know you're still in touch with him," Merrick said. "I saw the Christmas card you sent him on his coffee table last week. It's too bad things didn't work out between the two of you. You were so well-suited."

Casey turned away to check her pastry shell. Merrick trying

to make amends was almost as bad as Merrick putting her foot in her own mouth. Thank goodness she had chosen the Christmas card in question for its lack of a meaningful message. Merrick had probably peeked inside the card.

She opened the oven door and leaned in to prick a bubble of pastry with a fork, hoping the heat would explain her face. Since Kalin insisted on sending her cards at every excuse, along with occasional letters, she tried to reciprocate often enough to foster the idea that she regarded him as an old and dear friend.

Bonnie glanced at Casey. "It's Kalin's loss."

Casey steadied her reeling senses and crossed the white tile floor to the refrigerator with the cake layers. She returned to the table with a pound of butter and began heating another saucepan containing sugar and water.

"Anything between us was over years ago," she said. "After all, I was only eighteen then, and he was twenty-two. We both had lots of growing up to do."

Clay said, "I've always suspected McBryde wasn't all there." His eyes were fixed on Casey's face as she plugged in the electric mixer and began beating the butter.

Clay's obvious admiration couldn't help but lift Casey's spirits. She smiled at him and asked if he'd like to help her make the icing for the cake.

"Anything for you, babe. What do I do?"

Soon Clay was bending over the pan on the stove, monitoring the temperature of the candy thermometer Casey had placed in the boiling sugar syrup.

"We'll all help, Casey," Merrick said belatedly. "What can I do?"

"Could you bring me the cake layers in the fridge?"

Casey took the pan of syrup and poured it gradually into the butter with the electric mixer going full blast. The resulting frosting caused the three watching to squabble amicably over licking the bowl and the knife Casey used to spread the concoction over the cake. The cake gained almost an inch in height before she was through.

She had just accepted a taste of her own creation off Clay's finger when she noticed Bonnie staring rigidly at something in the doorway behind her. She turned to look as a deep, masculine voice said coolly, "Hello, Casey."

Casey froze and licked the icing carefully off her lips. "Hello, Kalin," she said slowly. "Fancy meeting you here."

Chapter 2

Kalin stared keenly at her, tight-lipped. He was six feet tall and had the easy, arrogant carriage of an athlete, and the tanned skin and steady gaze of an outdoorsman.

He stood just inside the door, dressed in dark trousers and a pale blue shirt open at the neck, and leaned against the doorjamb with the air of one who has come to stay a while.

Casey, who figured the only thing different about herself was her hairstyle, noted that although Kalin's physical attributes hadn't changed, something else had. The Kalin she'd known was open, honest, and loving. This man looked hard, almost intimidating.

She surveyed him, gave him a formal smile, and returned her attention to the knife full of frosting in her hand. The sight of him had caused a strange contraction in the vicinity of her heart and the feeling that her surroundings were whirling and closing in on her. It annoyed her because she thought she had prepared herself for this meeting.

"What brings you back to this country town?" Kalin asked. "I'm surprised there's anything here that attracts you."

Casey spread more frosting on her cake. "I'm surprised word hasn't traveled faster around this country town," she said. "My grandmother had a stroke two days ago. I came home to be with her."

Kalin's mouth twitched into a smile. "Is that so? I'm sorry about your grandmother. Now that you're home, she's liable to get well fast." He left the door and came toward her. "Let me look at you. How old are you now? Twenty-three? It doesn't seem possible. So you're now a professional chef. Well, well."

He came so close, Casey fancied she could feel the heat of his body. She had once associated Kalin with love and warmth.

She rushed into speech. "I understand you just sold your first book. Congratulations, Kalin."

His blue eyes scanned her "Thank you. It took a while, but it was worth it." He took his gaze off her long enough to look around the kitchen at the dishes remaining to be washed and the cake Casey was putting the finishing touches on. Then he added, "I figure that when I can average two books a year, I can quit practicing law."

"But you've only been in practice a couple of years," Clay exclaimed incredulously. "With your name . . . " He trailed off when Kalin cast him a look of impatient contempt.

"I never wanted to practice law in the first place," Kalin said, adding no explanation.

Bonnie was the only one to respond. "Too bad your Dad wasted all that money sending you to law school."

Kalin shifted to look down at the small brunette, his smile suddenly going crooked. "I always thought so."

Casey saw no reason to intervene. Let Kalin take care of himself, she reasoned, and evened off her frosting.

Clay, who had been staring at Kalin with an expression somewhere between contempt and disbelief, said suddenly, "I told you he wasn't all there."

Kalin's attention zeroed in on Clay with a vengeance. "Don't tell me you're one of those idiots who thinks a law degree is the key to success and status forever."

"It's a start," Clay returned. "Here, Casey, let me hold that pan. It's too heavy for you."

Casey glanced up in surprise. She had transferred her attention to the pastry shell, now cooled and ready for the filling she had set aside to cool in an ice bath.

She dried the water off the bottom of the pan. "I'd better do it myself. My wrists are stronger than they look."

The small group watched in silence as Casey poured the filling into the shell, spread it evenly, and began placing pecan halves in even, diagonal rows across the top.

"That's amazing, how fast you can do that," Bonnie said. "I'd spend an hour just on the pecans."

"It's not hard, once you've done it a few times." Casey finished the pecans, opened a jar of apple jelly, dumped a few spoonsful into a pan, and melted it.

Merrick, who hadn't said a word since Kalin's arrival, straightened, still staring at Kalin with disbelief. "I don't believe this. Five years."

Casey looked up from her pan, then back, conscious only of the necessity of concentrating very hard on her cooking. She couldn't begin to decipher the meaning buried in those words.

Kalin's thick brows drew together. "Yes, it has been five years, hasn't it? Believe me, I've been counting."

Merrick cleared her throat, nonplused. "Are you about done, Casey? I thought you said one hour."

Casey bit back a smile. "So I did. I decided to make a pecan tart to go with the cake. Sorry."

"Cheez, Merrick." Clay glanced at his phone. "It's only been an hour and fifteen minutes. Give us a break."

Merrick, brilliantly red, subsided.

Casey took pity on Merrick. "This is the final touch." She used a brush to spread the melted jelly over the pecans.

"That's spectacular." Clay cast a glance at Kalin. "One hour and twenty minutes. Where have you been all my life, sweetheart?"

Casey laughed. "In cooking school, where else?"

She caught the unsmiling, challenging stare Kalin directed at Clay and bit her lip to cover her shock. Apparently, old habits died hard with Kalin.

Merrick eyed the food with the attitude of one who scarcely knew what to do next. "How do we carry them?"

Clay lifted the gateau. "This cake is *light*."

"These are wonderful, Casey," Merrick said at last. "Thank you.

Don't you want to help serve them?"

"I'm sure you'll do a great job." Casey smiled graciously and carried the copper bowl to the sink.

Ordinarily she'd serve her own cooking, but Kalin had the look of a man who intended to help her. She needed to readjust to Kalin's physical presence slowly. No sense in overloading her circuits, she thought, smiling wryly.

Kalin came up behind her and leaned back against the counter so he could see her face. "Aren't you going to taste your own creations?"

Casey glanced up fleetingly. "I know what they taste like."

"Why don't you leave those dishes for Merrick? Consider it part of the general after-party clean-up she'll have to do."

Casey rinsed the bowl and reached for paper towels. "This is Mrs. Johnson's good copper bowl. I'd better clean it myself."

"I'll never understand this holy-holy attitude of cooks toward copper." He scanned her face, frowning. "If I know you, you traveled all night without a break, then waited on your grandmother all afternoon, and now you're going to cook for a crowd and clean up all the dishes."

Bonnie had risen and approached the sink. "Good for you, Kalin. She hasn't quit from the time she walked in the door."

"Here," Kalin said. "I'll finish the dishes. Sit down."

Casey, moved gently aside by Kalin, walked to a kitchen chair and pulled it out, then stood beside it watching Kalin unbutton his cuffs and roll up his sleeves. The breathless feeling in her chest intensified.

Bonnie stood ready to dry the dishes and put them away.

Casey decided to leave while she was ahead. She removed the big apron and rehung it, grabbed up her purse and jacket and headed for the door. She'd never dreamed her first meeting with Kalin after five years would go like this. She had proved she could face Kalin McBryde again, but she hadn't bargained for this rush of overwhelming feeling.

She'd expected innuendos or out-and-out contempt. Her worst-case scenario had included Kalin's expectation that she might fling herself at his feet once more. She hadn't been prepared for this resumption of his old protective attitude.

In the dining room, both items she had baked were surrounded by enthusiasts who had left only crumbs of each. She'd almost made it to the living room when Clay spotted her.

"You aren't leaving, are you?" he exclaimed, blocking her path. "This is the best cake I've ever eaten in my life, and you're the best looking professional chef I've ever seen. Tell me, babe, are you into lawyers?"

"Since when are you a lawyer, Rowe?" Kalin asked.

Casey whirled. He closed in on her fast, with his cuffs still rolled up, drying his hands on paper towels.

"As soon as I pass the bar exam," Clay said. "I already have a job lined up at Morgan, Brewster, and Kron."

"I had an offer to go there when I graduated. If that's where you plan to work, you aren't going to have time to pursue good-looking chefs. You'd better concentrate on your books."

"Is that why you turned them down?" Clay asked with contempt.

"Of course." Kalin grinned suddenly. "They wanted me to work weekends. Everyone knows I fish and hunt on the weekends. Come on, Casey. There's dancing in the den." He dropped the paper towels on the dining room table and took her arm.

Casey had no intention of dancing with Kalin. "Sorry. I was just leaving. It's been a long day."

"It's barely nine o'clock." Kalin's hand rested on her back in the old, familiar way.

"Maybe you'd like to sit out a dance with me before you go," Clay said wickedly, grinning at her.

"Tend to your own business, Rowe," Kalin snapped.

"This good-looking lady chef is now my business. Come along, babe. Let's get to know each other in the den."

Casey had no idea how things had escalated to the point where two rival males were squaring off. Kalin was about to throw a punch at Clay; she'd seen the signs often enough in the past.

"I really do have to go." She moved between the two men.

"Where's Merrick?"

"God knows," Clay said. "Is this clod putting you off lawyers, sweetheart?"

"I need to find Merrick," she said firmly. "I want to ask her about an application for law school before I leave."

"An application for law school?" Kalin repeated in open astonishment. "What on earth are you talking about?"

"She's decided to steal all your clients, McBryde," Clay said. "If you have any."

Kalin ignored Clay and took Casey's arm. "I thought culinary school was nirvana to you."

Casey stepped away from him, smiling. "I've decided to sue any cook daring to encroach upon one of my recipes."

A couple of small groups abandoned their discussions to watch the scene. Casey recognized several people who would remember her final, public breakup with Kalin.

"What?" Kalin looked baffled.

"Alienation of affection." Casey said, choosing words at random. "Like most Americans, I've grown litigious. Only I'm too cheap to pay a lawyer. I'd rather become a lawyer myself."

This statement resulted in a spattering of laughter from around the living room.

Kalin grinned and closed in on her once more. "You've come to the right place. I'm very into alienation of affection suits. Let's talk about it in the den."

"I prefer to talk to Merrick out here." Casey backed away. "She promised to help me apply."

"So I'll put on a wig and take the LSAT for you," Kalin promised, still smiling. "Come on."

The image of Kalin wearing a wig and taking the Law School Admission Test in her place almost overset Casey's gravity.

"You'd look cute in a wig, McBryde," one man called.

Kalin didn't take his eyes off Casey. "I'd pass the bar exam for her on the first try, too." He took her arm before she could hide it behind her back.

People hooted and laughed. Judging from the comments, the speaker had just flunked the bar exam.

Kalin guided Casey through the living room and into the darkened den, where he seated her on a small sofa. Taking her belongings, he placed them in the corner and sat beside her, his long, hard thigh pressed tightly against hers.

A stereo played dance tunes for the few couples who cared to dance in the darkened den. Casey took several deep breaths and stared around the room. It was almost unchanged from the time she and Kalin had used dancing as an excuse to exchange kisses at a similar party when she was in high school.

"Law school?" Kalin asked in a gentle voice.

"Actually, it was a joke." Casey searched for her purse. "I'd better be going."

The search gave her an excuse to avoid looking at him. She wished he'd move aside so he wouldn't be touching her.

"Not yet. I want to dance with you. For old times' sake. Where did you meet Clayton Rowe?"

He sounded jealous, but that was impossible.

"In the kitchen." She found her purse, tucked it back under her arm, and slid to the edge of the sofa.

Kalin removed it and stood, bringing her up with him as he dropped the purse on the sofa.

"Dance with me," he said, and took her in his arms.

Her defenses went into shock as Kalin moved her slowly to the music. He pressed her against his hard, warm body despite her initial attempts to maintain her distance. The scent of his woodsy aftershave filled her senses and the steadily tightening pressure of his arm around her waist created a feeling in her that was somewhere between terror and longing.

He shouldn't have this much power over her after all this time, she thought, dazed. It was unfair.

"What took you so long to come home?" Kalin asked softly.

"I've been busy." She lifted her head from the temptation of his shoulder. "Tell me some more about your book. I was thrilled to hear you'd sold it."

Once, Kalin would have talked for hours with that invitation. "You should be. I used all your suggestions in rewriting it. Would you like a cut of the royalties?"

"No, thanks." Casey stiffened and remembered how he had accused her of being out for what she could get. In spite of her control, some of the emotion she felt ravaged her voice.

"What have I said?" Kalin rubbed his hand across her back.

"Nothing." She moved back. "I'd better be going."

"Take it easy," he said with maddening gentleness. "I only want to dance with you. After Merrick went through all the trouble to set this up, we don't want to disappoint her."

Heat flooded her face. "She's yours to please, not mine."

"Ssshhh. She'll hear you."

His whisper was stagy in the extreme, and Casey knew Merrick stood in the doorway watching them.

Unbidden, a memory rose in Casey's mind, of herself clinging to Kalin's arm and tearfully begging him not to leave her like that. Merrick had hovered nearby, avidly watching the scene.

She turned her face away from the door.

Kalin executed a fancy step that took them behind another couple. "What are you thinking about?" he asked in stern tones.

She jerked her attention back, feeling his touch all the way to her bones, and lowered her eyes before they encountered his. "Nothing you'd find interesting. By the way, Merrick is very concerned that you aren't upholding the family tradition."

"I've noticed. Now that I'm an unimportant lawyer, she finally avoids introducing me as her cousin who's going to be as important as his famous father." He invited her to laugh with him as he drew her close once more.

Casey obliged with a perfunctory smile. "She wanted to know what I had done to you."

"What you had done to me?" Kalin repeated and chuckled. "It was the other way around, I think. I drove you into leaving Winnie at least two months before you planned, didn't I?"

Casey drew her sagging dignity around her like a shawl. "I decided to leave early before things got even more unpleasant." Where was her sense of humor when she needed it? Gone into shock, no doubt, along with the rest of her faculties.

"Don't you think you were overreacting?"

At that, Casey tried vainly to put some distance between them. "Watch yourself, Kalin. If you're not careful, I'll get my hooks into you again. I'm on the lookout for a man destined to become either a bestselling author or a rich criminal lawyer whose best clients are Mafia dons."

Kalin, rather than snapping back at her in kind, responded with genuine laughter, which had every head not already watching them turning their way.

"Now that is the clearest, most succinct summary of my father's career that I have ever been privileged to hear, except that most of his money came from drug smugglers."

Casey, confused, stumbled over his foot and had to hold on to him to right herself. "Whatever. On the other hand, maybe I'd better go after Clayton Rowe. *He* wouldn't stick at defending a drug smuggler or a murderer."

"Forget it. Think of the challenge in prodding me into working weekends and taking on cases I'd rather avoid."

Kalin suddenly brimmed over with the joy of living. The hard, closed-in expression of earlier had vanished.

"That would be a challenge beyond my modest capabilities. I'm out of prodding and into relaxation."

"Be reasonable, Casey." Kalin's low laughter as he swung her around to a beat of the music annoyed her further. "Doesn't fishing count as relaxation anymore? Or has it been so long since you've held a fishing pole that you've forgotten how?"

These words conjured up memories of Kalin teaching her to set hooks, run crab nets, and watch the tip of a fishing pole with his arm around her. "I'm now into things that don't require mosquito repellant or chicken necks."

"When Uncle Jack sees you, he's probably going to write you a prescription for a fishing trip. When was the last time you slept a full eight hours, or read a good book?"

The implications of these questions, after she'd spent time and effort over her makeup and hair for this occasion, disheartened her. "I had—have a high stress job in New York."

Kalin caught the nuance. "So how long are you planning to stay in Winnie?"

"That depends on Granny. Several weeks, a few months. I don't know yet."

"I see you still overwork yourself to the point of collapse," he said.

The music stopped, and Casey backed away. Kalin kept a hand at her waist and urged her to sit once more on the sofa.

"I'd like to take you to dinner tomorrow night," he said slowly. "Do you think—"

"I'm afraid that's impossible," Casey interrupted, nerves jittering. "But thank you all the same. I'm going to be taking care of Granny and doing a lot of other things."

"Look at me, Casey."

She winced. Kalin was probably beginning to realize she hadn't looked him directly in the face at all that evening, except for the one straightforward glance she had accorded him when he first walked into the kitchen.

She looked up and focused on his nose.

Kalin studied her a moment in the semi-darkness. "Don't treat me like a polite stranger. Yell at me if you want to. I probably deserve it."

"You want me to scream at the top of my voice that I wouldn't go with you to a crawdad race?" She got her fingers on her purse and clutched it in her lap.

"If that's the way you feel about it, why not?" He watched her closely.

"I don't feel quite that dramatic about it. The best way to phrase it is that my current list of priorities does not include dinner with you. Sorry if that isn't dramatic enough for you."

Kalin laughed softly and reached for her hand. "I think it's only fair to warn you that you're going to have to rearrange your priorities. I'll pick you up tomorrow night at seven."

Casey contemplated scurrying back to New York.

"If you aren't at home," Kalin warned, "I'll come looking for you at the hospital."

He would, too, which was just what Granny needed. Now Casey was doubly annoyed. "Don't bother. I may not be there."

It was one thing to send Kalin impersonal Christmas cards from a distance. It was quite another to sit anywhere within touching distance of him.

"Then I'll wait there until you turn up, however long it takes."

She'd better get tough, or he'd soon know all he had to do was touch her and she'd probably melt at his feet again.

"Kalin, I will not go to dinner with you tomorrow night or any other night. I'll be very busy while I'm here, so don't ask anymore, okay? I have to go."

Kalin didn't seem to hear her. "How about dancing with me one more time?"

Casey got to her feet, cramming her arms into her jacket sleeves willy-nilly. She didn't need Kalin's warm hands on her, even to help her on with her jacket.

He moved to block her path. "I need to talk to you, Casey. I'd rather do it over a good dinner somewhere, but if you're going to be like this, any place will do. Just be ready tomorrow night at seven."

Casey didn't trust herself to reply. She walked around him, out of the den, and through the living room to the door.

Bonnie caught her near the front door. "How about lunch tomorrow at Cap'n Bob's?"

"You're on." Casey caught Kalin's approach out of the corner of her eye. She dropped her voice. "Meet you there at noon."

Bonnie looked over Casey's shoulder, grinned, and stepped aside.

Casey swept regally out the front door, deeming it a waste of time to seek out Merrick. Besides, she didn't need another confrontation between Kalin, who seemed to think he had some sort of right to her, and Clayton Rowe, who welcomed a challenge.

"Slow down, will you?" Kalin stayed on her heels. "If you stumble in those high heels—"

Casey stepped on a lump in the shell-covered, circular drive, staggered, and felt Kalin's arms come around her, pulling her up swiftly against his hard chest. Shaken, she clutched him.

"You shouldn't rush around on uneven ground like this if you're going to wear those heels. What's your hurry? Are you afraid I'm going to steal a kiss?"

Since he held her against him, and her pulses and nervous system raised riot up and down her body, that was precisely what she feared. "That's the least of my worries right now. I've been away from the telephone too long. The hospital might have tried to call. Excuse me, please."

"Better put it at the top of your list." He used one hand to turn up her chin and the other to hold her against him, with unmistakable intent. "Right along with getting a cell phone and giving me the number."

He kissed her, and Casey felt the entire universe shift beneath her already unsteady feet. Although he kept the kiss gentle and unhurried, he seemed intent upon marking every bit of her mouth as his own. And she felt so stunned, she stood there a moment and let him get away with it, until she suddenly snapped back into reality and realized what she was doing.

She shoved him away, terrified that she would give herself away if she allowed the kiss to last another second, and marched to the little beige car she had rented in Houston.

Kalin followed and stood a few feet from her while she unlocked the car door and got in, slamming the door emphatically. He tapped on the window until she rolled it down.

"Seven tomorrow night," he said.

"I'm can't go. I've got to start priming my brain for the LSAT."

Casey ground the starter, gunned the motor, and kicked up a spray of shell as she pulled out onto the highway. She had been kidding herself—she wasn't as ready to face Kalin McBryde as she'd thought.

But then, she had expected anything and everything other than this single-minded pursuit he'd started.

And she'd thought she would no longer respond to him as she had when she was eighteen and had loved him with all her heart.

Casey drove the two miles down the quiet, sparsely populated road to the old farmhouse among the rice fields where she'd grown up and remembered the way Kalin had pursued her when they'd first met at the Rice Festival. After he'd carried her cooking contest entries inside for her, she'd found him beside her all day.

When she'd spoken of analyzing her chief rival's entry, Kalin had braved the wrath of the cook and stole her a big chunk.

When she'd ridden the Ferris wheel, he'd climbed into the seat beside her and wanted to know why she was ignoring him.

He hadn't left her side until she agreed to go out with him, and it looked as though he was using the same method again.

The old house still had the odor of a house that had been shut up for several days. Granny's neat kitchen was old-fashioned but functional. The ancient refrigerator made strange sounds, but it cooled to the degree a trained chef required. The stove was an elderly gas range, but it had all the functions she needed.

Alice Gray was finding it difficult to eat since her illness. Casey set a carton of eggs out on the table, along with sugar and milk.

Before she went to bed, she'd make custard cups topped with real caramel that would tempt Alice's flagging appetite, especially when served on one of her own Blue Willow plates with a flower beside it.

The kitchen telephone rang while she beat the eggs.

"Casey?" It was Kalin. "I just wanted to be sure you got home safely. Are you all right?"

"Yes, I'm fine, thank you," she replied in her politest tones. "It was kind of you to call."

Kalin laughed. In the background, she could hear Christmas music and people talking.

"It wasn't kind, and you know it. Can I come over?"

"I'm about to go to bed," she said, startled.

"No, you aren't. You're baking something for somebody. Get to bed, Casey. You look worn to the bone."

She would have to take steps, she realized, or Kalin would know she had quit her job with no intentions of returning. Trust Kalin to complicate a life she was determined to simplify.

"Thanks a lot," she grumbled. "It was a big hassle, getting off work and packing."

"Just so you aren't too busy unpacking tomorrow night at seven," he said, and hung up before she could refuse to go out with him.

Casey slammed the phone down. She'd never, *never* been able to get the last word in on Kalin McBryde.

One of these days, she thought furiously, sifting flour.

She could only hope that the people eating her cooking tomorrow wouldn't detect any residual vibrations left in the food from her emotions tonight.

Chapter 3

The next morning Casey found young John Broussard, a man in his mid-fifties whose father had enjoyed the same name, finishing up chores in the barn after turning the old plow horse, Cork, and Alice Gray's milk cow, Eloise, out into the pasture beside the barn. He was happy to accept the neatly boxed, freshly baked cake she held out to him as a thank you for all his hard work.

"I remember that bread you used to give us when you were just a kid," he said. "I wish my wife would take up baking like that."

Casey kept her gaze away from his expansive middle and said tactfully, "Not everyone enjoys cooking."

On her way back to the house, Casey stopped by the chicken yard and tossed the twelve hens and one large, New Hampshire Red rooster more scratch grain.

"Your chickens miss you, Granny," she said, as she entered her grandmother's room at the small community hospital carrying a large box. "The rooster doesn't know me and kept warning the hens away when I put down their feed."

Alice Gray focused on her granddaughter with difficulty. "Isn't it early, yet? You should be resting from your trip. Don't you know it's Sunday? I didn't raise you to work on the Sabbath." She glared at Casey's jeans and sweatshirt with faded blue eyes. "I want you going to church this morning. I'll bet you haven't been inside a church since you left." Her voice sounded slurred and querulous. "You can tell me about the sermon afterwards."

"I told you I'd cook you something special. Do you want it now, or have you just had breakfast?" Casey set the box down and regarded her grandmother with concern.

"I can't eat the food they serve you in here. It isn't what I'm used to," Alice said in plaintive tones.

"I know, Granny. That's why I made you something I know you used to like."

Casey busied herself at the bedside table then pushed it around so Alice could admire the effect of the custard cup with its shiny caramel coating turned out onto one of her own china plates. An oak branch from the big oak tree in the back yard sat in a vase beside the plate.

Alice's face brightened, although she was careful not to sound too enthusiastic. "I believe I could eat a bite of that."

Casey fed her grandmother the entire custard, even scraping out the container for the remains of the caramel. When she had finished, Alice Gray drifted into the drowsy state she remained in much of the time, and Casey awaited the arrival of Dr. Jack Johnson, Merrick's father and her grandmother's physician, in the hall outside Alice's room.

"Casey Gray," the doctor exclaimed when Casey greeted him. "My wife said you must be back in town. Her copper bowl is shining like a new penny, and my nephew is spending the weekend and behaving like he sat on a fire ant mound."

Jack Johnson was a short man with receding blond hair, kind brown eyes, and the weathered skin of an avid fisherman. He had been Casey's physician all through her school years, and treated Kalin more like a son than Kalin's own father had.

"How is Granny, Dr Johnson? I never saw her sick in bed all the time I lived at home." Alice Gray's stillness frightened Casey. She could not visualize Alice confined to a bed.

"It was a bad stroke, I'm afraid, Casey. There will be some permanent damage to her right side, but we're hopeful she can begin some physical therapy soon." He went into a technical description of what the illness involved, and finished with, "You may want to transfer her to a hospital in Beaumont or Houston, where the facilities for treatment will be much greater."

Casey, more disturbed than ever, said slowly, "She's already told me that if I send her away from you and all her friends here, she'll just go ahead and die."

"Then keep her here," Dr. Johnson said, eying Casey's troubled face. "Now, tell me about yourself. When was the last time you cooked something and ate it yourself?"

"I'm tired of my own cooking," Casey grumbled.

His gaze grew sharper, taking in the faint hollows beneath her cheekbones and the look of strain no amount of makeup could hide. "What's troubling you, Casey? You look as though you haven't rested well in some time."

Casey shrugged. "I had a high stress job in New York. I'll probably feel better as soon as I've rested from the trip."

Or else, she thought with fatalistic humor. She had loved her work, but she stayed too keyed up to rest. Then when she actually achieved any rest, it was troubled by dreams of Kalin.

"You've always had the worst qualities of a workaholic. You should get my nephew to take you fishing. You can use my boat."

"Dr. Johnson, the last thing I want to do is go fishing with Kalin McBryde. If you could find an excuse to send him back to Houston, I'll be forever grateful."

"In that case, I'll have to take you myself," he said with aplomb. "There's nothing like fishing to relax the nerves and rejuvenate the body. In fact, I'll write you a prescription to that effect. Consider it preventative medicine." He actually brought forth a prescription pad, scribbled a few words on it, and passed it to her.

"Be ready Wednesday afternoon," he said. "It's my afternoon off. We'll go to the lake."

Casey took the paper and attempted to decipher the scratches on it. "This could say anything."

"It says what I say it says." Dr. Johnson smiled at her. "Of all the patients I see who could be cured by a fishing trip, you're the worst. A fulminating case, my dear young lady."

35

Casey watched him enter her grandmother's room and sit beside her bed a few moments, checking her speech, studying her chart, and making a few notations.

Dr. Johnson, it was said, had cured more patients with fishing trips than he had with medicine, although in this case, she suspected him of matchmaking. She hoped he read her loud and clear when it came to Kalin.

Casey drove back down the sunny highway to church after changing into one of her wool business suits. The sermon almost passed over her head, however, as memories of how Kalin had appeared beside her at the church's harvest service the day after she met him intruded. She had thought him the handsomest man she'd ever seen.

She brought herself back to the sermon by admonishing herself that she'd been only sixteen at the time. Her experience had been extremely limited.

She went out to the parking lot with several old friends and was shocked to see Kalin standing beside a navy blue SUV that contained several fishing poles and an assortment of other fishing equipment.

Casey stared, remembering the red sports car Kalin had almost driven into the ground when she knew him. "What a come-down for your image," she said, detaching herself from the group. She had to face him some time, she lectured inwardly, studying the center of his forehead.

"Actually, this is what I wanted all along." Kalin smiled and came toward her. "Dad thought all college guys needed a fast sports car. Since he was buying in those days, I had to take what he gave me or walk."

"He could have saved a lot of money on one of these over that red Viper of yours," she commented, and pretended to study the church building and the grounds.

"He wasn't interested in saving money. He was interested in bribing me to graduate at the top of my class."

"And did you?"

"I made the top half," Kalin said, grinning. He gestured at the SUV. His sleeves were rolled up to reveal tanned, muscular forearms. "Want to try it out?"

"Sorry. I'm meeting Bonnie for lunch in five minutes, then I have to get back to the hospital."

She smiled coolly and unlocked the door to her car, conscious of a drumming in her ears. The sight of those arms and his long, slender hands reminded her far too vividly of the way they contrasted with her own pale skin.

Kalin didn't seem unduly disturbed. "Don't you have anything to wear but those dark wool suits?"

"Of course." Kalin had never complained about her clothes in the old days. "How would you like it if I asked if all you had to wear were plaid flannel shirts and jeans?"

Kalin laughed. "I'd reply that it was, but for you, I'll rush out and buy one of those pinstriped success suits."

She opened her car door and got in, then rolled down the window when he gestured at her. "Yes?"

"Shall I rush out and buy a suit? I'm picking you up tonight at seven, you know. If flannel shirts and jeans aren't good enough for you—"

"Wear whatever you like, but don't bother showing up at seven or at any other time. I'm busy preparing for the LSAT."

"You've had a rough morning at the hospital," Kalin observed sympathetically.

Casey backed her car out. One thing she didn't need from Kalin McBryde was sympathy. Another was a dinner date.

She shot down the highway to Cap'n Bob's Cajun Cooking, wondering at the furious thundering of her heart. Was she actually thinking of being ready at seven? Perhaps she should make an appointment with a good psychiatrist.

She hardened her heart. In another day or two, Kalin would decide she wasn't worth the bother and go back to Houston. When he did, she'd find some way to celebrate. She so did not need this, when her life was already in such turmoil.

The popular Cajun restaurant where Casey had spent her high school years working as the evening cook still occupied the same tin building, but in the space beside the back entrance where Captain Bob had once parked his old Buick a new black pickup truck shone like a diamond in the white shell parking lot.

The new truck ought to mean the restaurant was doing well, although there weren't nearly as many cars in the parking lot as there should have been on a Sunday after church. Casey walked to the double set of glass doors that marked the entrance and noted greasy handprints on the glass.

Bonnie already had a table near the front window. "Isn't this a hoot? I haven't been here but once or twice since you left, and let me tell you, it isn't the same."

Casey stood beside her chair a moment and studied the big dining room, with its red-checked tablecloths and vases of plastic flowers. The mural of a Louisiana bayou complete with Spanish moss and alligators that covered one entire wall received special consideration.

She sat down. "I can see it isn't. I'd hate to know when was the last time they cleaned that mural, not to mention these phony flowers." Casey picked up the menu and regarded it nostalgically.

"What are you having?" Bonnie refolded her menu.

"It says here they have farm-raised redfish, blackened in the true Cajun manner. We'll see." Casey folded the menu and laid it down to twist in her chair and stare meaningfully at the window opening to the kitchen.

"Captain Bob had to retire a couple of years ago. Bad health, or so they say. Joe is running the business now." Bonnie wiggled her eyebrows. "Joe just doesn't have the personality his dad had. In fact, people say Joe is gone more than he's here."

"A girl, no doubt." Casey recalled the time Joe Kerns had

fought Kalin one night in the parking lot when Kalin first started taking her out.

Joe had adored Casey from afar for several years but never asked her out until Kalin appeared on the scene. Then his resentment of the situation overcame his judgment, and Kalin had taken pleasure in pointing out the errors in Joe's ways.

"When the owner of a business is in love, the help follows suit," she added. Her gaze focused on the small window that opened into the kitchen, where a lanky youth in a white smock and chef's hat exchanged views with a waitress.

By the time their waitress arrived, Casey had subjected the entire restaurant to an expert's scrutiny and reached a conclusion. "Captain Bob was the soul of this place," she told Bonnie. "Joe needs to do something fast. I remember when this restaurant had standing room only on Sundays after church."

The waitress stood beside their table, chewing gum and tapping her pencil on her pad. She eyed Casey's creamy silk blouse and tailored suit admiringly. "You used to work here?"

"I was the evening cook," Casey said. "Captain Bob ran this place the way he ran his tugboat crew. Everything was in place and polished."

"I never met him," the waitress said. "Take your order?"

Bonnie didn't laugh until the girl had returned to the kitchen window. "I'm glad I thought of asking you here. It's been worth it, seeing you in action."

"Oh, I'm not in action, Bonnie. If I were, this place would be straightened out by this afternoon."

Bonnie grinned. "I believe you." She paused. "It looks like old Kalin McBryde would like you to straighten him out, too."

"There's nothing wrong with Kalin that I'm able to help." Casey squashed the image of Kalin's lean, muscular body as he stood beside his vehicle.

Bonnie sipped water. "You realize he still cares for you, don't you?"

Casey gasped inwardly and tried to keep her poise. "He can't possibly. He hasn't even seen me in five years. The things he said . . . ," she trailed off.

"Don't you think you might be dwelling too much on what he said? Whatever it was, he probably didn't mean it, you know. You should give him another chance, Casey. You might be surprised."

"I can guarantee you, I'd be surprised. I couldn't think about that scene for years afterward without wanting to die."

"You can have the benefit of my reasonably unbiased opinion if you care to tell all." Bonnie propped her chin on her hand and looked across the table invitingly. "What did he say that you find so hard to forgive and forget?"

Casey had never told anyone what Kalin had said during the two-week period their relationship had been lurching toward its finale. She still cringed with shame whenever she thought of them, and found it difficult to contemplate developing a relationship with another man because of them.

Deep within her, a voice warned that the real reason she couldn't develop an interest in other men was because they weren't Kalin, but Casey knew that was ridiculous. Now that she had faced him successfully, she could get on with her life.

Bonnie added, "I know he said you were trying to trap him into marriage the way your mother tried to trap your father, but that wasn't what made you run. You're still running, if you want my opinion."

Casey flushed and kept her eyes on her water glass. If she talked about it, the hurt would drain away and she could begin to heal. Or so they said.

Why was it so difficult to begin?

"Well, he did say I was trying to trick him into making love to me," she said at last. "Which was true enough. I used to think I'd die if he didn't, I wanted him so badly. What hurt was that he made fun of the way I responded when he touched me. He said I behaved like a bitch in heat."

"Kalin said that?" Bonnie stared.

"Yes, he did." Stated flatly, it sounded silly, and it sounded incredible to anyone who knew Kalin. "I couldn't believe it. I couldn't out-talk him, with his talent for using words, so I cried and begged him to . . ." She trailed off and shrugged. "Well, you know about that. He was so angry. So disgusted and fed up with me. And suddenly, everything I felt seemed cheap. What made me feel so ashamed was the way I begged him—in public, the way my mother had begged my father."

She was still ashamed, Casey realized, and she was frightened to sense that her physical response to Kalin would be the same if she allowed him to get too close.

"Casey Gray, you've blown this whole thing all out of proportion," Bonnie said. "You know good and well he didn't mean all that. I don't know what got into him then, but I do know he regrets it now."

"Probably," Casey agreed. "Who wants to have to remember saying things like that to someone whose major crime was loving you too much?"

She connected two drops of water that had formed on her water glass with her finger. The humiliation had gone so deep, she still found it difficult to think about. She had never connected the way she responded to Kalin with her mother's pregnancy and public pleas—until Kalin had pointed it out in scathing tones.

Casey had been on her cell phone at the time, begging Kalin to please just listen to her. When he'd hung up in her ear after speaking his mind on the subject, she had immediately ended her cell phone service and donated the phone to a battered women's charity.

After that, she'd rather have died than speak to Kalin McBryde for any reason. She never wanted to look him in the face again. She didn't buy another cell phone until several weeks after she arrived at her culinary school, and she had instructed her grandparents not to give the number to Kalin, even if by some miracle he asked for it.

"I expect his father's death was rough on him." Bonnie regarded her with sympathy. "I don't know what went wrong when old Walter McBryde died, but you can bet it was strictly bad news for Kalin. For the McBrydes to go from rich to ordinary within a span of a few months, something bad must have happened. You were still going with Kalin then—didn't he ever say anything?"

Casey shook her head. Memories surfaced, of Kalin's stunned blue eyes and the way he had wanted to spend hours just holding her after his father's funeral.

All she knew was that Walter McBryde had died suddenly of a massive heart attack. Kalin had supposedly inherited great wealth, but it seemed, from the little he'd said, that what he really inherited was trouble.

"All the same, you should let him explain if he wants to," Bonnie said.

Casey kept her eyes on the design she was drawing in the condensation on her water glass. "I don't want his explanations."

"Casey, listen to me. What can it hurt to hear his side of the story? The trouble with you is you're judging yourself by what Kalin said without considering how rational his judgment was at the time." Bonnie waited a moment to let this digest, then added, "Do you remember how mad Kalin used to get because you wouldn't take a day off from work every now and then to go places with him?"

"Rich kids have a hard time understanding what it's like for us poor kids who have to work."

"Kalin wasn't like that, and you know it. What made him mad was your attitude about it. You always gave the impression that the world would end if you didn't earn every possible dollar."

"I had to save for culinary school," Casey defended herself. "Grandpa couldn't afford to send me."

"I'm just pointing out that Kalin could have gotten fed up because of other things, chiefly that attitude of yours about working yourself half to death. It used to worry him. Do you know, you were the only girl in our class who never in her life had a tan? The rest of us were religious about hitting the beach. Not you. You were either at Cap'n Bob's or baking in your own kitchen for anyone in town who'd lost a relative."

Casey sat in silence a moment then said, "You're probably right, Bonnie. I'll think about it."

"Do that. And don't, for God's sake, fall for Clayton Rowe. The only thing he's really interested in is getting one up on Kalin." She paused for impact. "Kalin was the only person at the party last night who tried to help you with the unglamorous part of your cooking—the dishes. You should pay some attention to that instead of a temporary aberration on his part."

Casey broke into helpless laughter. "I love it when you start laying down the law to me. A temporary aberration. That's good. Did you learn that at the beauty school?"

"I wish you could have seen the way he looked at you last night before you knew he was standing there. He was literally feasting on you with his eyes."

"That conjures up an unfortunate mental image to a cook," Casey said, still chuckling.

"I'm your best friend, remember? Your interests are my interests. You still care about Kalin, don't you." It was a statement of fact, not a question.

"No way," Casey said swiftly. "I still have a lot of feelings tied up with him that I need to sort out. My pride seems to be the main thing involved at the moment."

"Yeah, you always did have lots of pride," Bonnie agreed. "Too much. Do you think you could sink it just once so he can get close enough to apologize?"

"He apologized years ago," Casey said, recalling the letter Kalin had written her within a few weeks of her departure. "I accepted. That's all there was to it."

"You never told me that," Bonnie accused. "You never told me you send him Christmas cards, either."

"There was nothing to tell. He sends me Christmas cards and Valentine cards and St. Patrick's Day cards. So every now and then I send him one."

"To make him think you aren't holding a grudge," Bonnie said, with shrewd insight.

"I'm not holding a grudge. I just don't feel the need to stay in touch with him, that's all. I have nothing to say to him." Her water tasted like soap. She set it down and glared at the glass. "Can you blame me? Anything I'd written in any card would have been broadcast all over town by now."

Bonnie laughed. "Good old Merrick. Casey, you've got to talk to Kalin. It's the only way you'll be able to let it go."

"I have let go." Casey smiled. "I think you're trying to get me to move back to Winnie."

"Can you blame me? I miss you, Casey. If I thought you were having a good time in New York, I'd say more power to you. But you aren't. I've never gotten the impression that you liked anything about it. The truth is, you're a small town Southeast Texas girl trapped in the big city, and it's eating you alive. When Dr. Johnson sees you—"

"I saw him this morning," Casey said, grinning. "He's taking me fishing Wednesday afternoon."

"Hah. That means the condition is life-threatening."

"No, it doesn't. Dr. Johnson just likes to fish."

"He cures people on those fishing trips," Bonnie said darkly. "Even tough cases like yours."

Casey grinned. "I can't wait." She looked around the restaurant. "I'm going to speak to the manager if we don't get some food pretty soon. This is ridiculous."

"That's why Cap'n Bob's has lost business." Bonnie's gaze focused on something outside the window. "It's like this all the time. Well, well. Look who's here."

Casey followed Bonnie's line of vision and saw Kalin slam the door of his SUV and head toward the front entrance.

Immediately her heart shifted into overdrive at the sight of his tall, masculine form, and she wondered if pride alone could cause the upheaval in her nervous system.

Aloud, she said, "It's a good thing we chose a table for two. He'll have to sit somewhere else."

But Kalin, who spotted them at once, dragged up a chair from another table and seated himself at the edge of their table.

"Since I'm probably the topic of conversation," he said, eyes gleaming, "I thought I'd come help you two discuss me better."

"No such luck," Bonnie said. "Casey is giving me a blow-by-blow description of what's wrong with this place and what should be done to fix it."

Kalin glanced around, folding his arms on the table. "I haven't been in here since the last time I picked Casey up here. It looks more or less the same. A little dingier, perhaps."

"A lot dingier." Casey studied the floor in an attempt to block out the sight of Kalin's arms. "That's part of what's wrong with it. Take that floor, for instance."

"Ugh," Bonnie said. "Let's talk about something pleasant, like the fact that Christmas will be here in a few days."

"Who could forget it, with that ghastly Christmas music playing in the background?" Casey looked for their waitress. "It should either be turned off or switched to a decent station."

"Stop giving the evil eye to the employees." Kalin reached out to tap her hand. "What do you want for Christmas?"

Casey blinked. No one had asked her that question in years. "I want Granny to get well and come home." She refused to let Bonnie catch her eye. "Besides, we never celebrated Christmas, or even had a Christmas tree. Grandpa thought it had lost all its proper meaning."

"Yes, I remember," Kalin said. "You and your grandmother used to celebrate Old Christmas on January sixth."

Casey recalled spending Old Christmas Eve with Kalin in the barn, waiting until midnight to see if the animals would kneel out of respect for the Christ child. The hour of midnight passed them by entirely, so engrossed they had been in each other.

She glanced fleetingly at Kalin then shifted her gaze once more to their waitress. He remembered also, if the taut expression on his face was anything to go by.

"Casey Gray," a male voice exclaimed. "I can't believe it."

Kalin glanced back, then at Casey with narrowed eyes.

Casey smiled brilliantly at her former co-worker, Joe Kerns. "Hi, Joe. I was going to see if you were in before I left. You remember Bonnie and Kalin, don't you? How is your father?"

Joe smiled at Bonnie, nodded with bare politeness at Kalin, and said, "Not too well, I'm afraid. He had to move to Arizona. His lungs, you know. Say, Casey, do you have a minute?"

"It looks like it," Casey said. "The service is a little slow this morning. Do you mind, Bonnie?"

Kalin said nothing but his face made his feelings plain even to Joe, who flushed with embarrassment.

Casey found it hard to credit the changes in Joe. When she left, he had been a big, clumsy boy with an ingenuous face, untamed sandy hair, and plain clothes. He'd ridden bulls and broncos and dreamed of going on the rodeo circuit someday.

Now he sported full Western gear, including an enormous gold nugget belt buckle, and his hair had been professionally styled. She had no doubt that Joe owned the black pickup she had seen parked outside.

Joe led the way to his office, a small, crowded room near the end of a short hallway that also housed the restrooms.

"Actually, the service is what I wanted to talk to you about," he said. "Do you need a job while you're in town?"

Casey studied the untidy stacks of bills on Joe's desk, mixed with packing slips, newspapers, and magazines. Captain Bob Kerns had kept that desk in strict order.

"What did you have in mind, Joe? Do you need another cook?"

Joe watched her with a hopeful expression. "Actually, I need someone to run the place for a while. Could you do that?"

"My grandmother—"

"I understand," Joe cut in. "You wouldn't have to be here every minute. I never am. The employees know what to do, so you'd just need to oversee things."

Casey had her own ideas about that, but she kept them to herself. "I don't know. I'll have to talk to Granny."

Alice Gray had already made her thoughts plain. She flatly refused to have Casey spending every minute at the hospital. It annoyed her, and Casey's constant presence would interfere with the long afternoon visits of Alice's friends.

To Casey, accustomed to working twelve to sixteen hour days, the prospect of empty afternoons was appalling.

Another thought struck her: the job would give her the perfect excuse to avoid Kalin McBryde until she could sort out the tangled maze of emotions she felt in his presence.

"On second thought, I'll do it," she said. "So long as you understand why I can't be here at all times. We can discuss it further this afternoon. I need to get back to my friends."

"I was surprised to see that McBryde fellow with you," Joe said, eyes on his desk. "I heard he was pretty rough on you back before you left town."

Casey shrugged and said nothing.

Joe grinned and added, "Heck, when I remember how he threatened me, I was surprised to hear the way he dumped you. Is he really going to marry Sunny Cansler?"

Casey's heart skipped a beat. "I don't know, Joe. Who's Sunny Cansler?"

"Some bleached blond from Houston. I saw her with him at the rodeo last year. Someone said they were getting married."

Casey struggled to beat back the roaring blackness that

threatened to close in on her. "Maybe so. Better her than me."

Joe laughed. "Say, what's this I hear about law school?"

After living five years in big cities where people took no particular interest in her, Casey had forgotten the swiftness with which news spread in small rural communities.

"Well, Joe, I've decided Merrick Johnson has the right idea. In order to be a truly patriotic American, I need to sue the pants off as many of my fellow citizens as possible."

"No kidding." Joe regarded her with respect. "Pop always said you were smarter than he was when it came to the business end of the restaurant."

She became conscious that Joe's attention had riveted on something behind her and knew Kalin stood in the door.

"In fact, I have a whole new goal in life," she added. "Outdoing Kalin McBryde in law school."

Chapter 4

Casey made no attempt to speak as she started back to the table, followed closely by Kalin.

"Slow down," he said. "In case you're worried, I'm not marrying Sunny Cansler. She's an old family friend."

His voice rode a fine line between sarcasm and laughter, and he grasped her arm and pulled her to a halt before she could reach the dining room.

"I'm not worried," she said in much the same tone he had used. "In fact, I was prepared to offer you my congratulations."

That gave her a fair idea of how long he had been standing there listening before Joe noticed his presence.

"You're too kind. What did Joe want?"

"He wanted to ask my advice on something. Bonnie is waiting." Her heart began to pound erratically, and she tried to withdraw her arm from his hold.

He tightened his clasp. "Casey, I want to talk to you."

She met his intense gaze for a fraction of a second in the dimly lit hallway. "Bonnie is waiting." She jerked her arm free with a desperate motion. "Some other time, maybe."

"Tonight, then." He made no attempt to argue with her and followed her across the dining room.

"I told you, Kalin, I'm busy. I don't have time to run around the way I did when I was a teenager."

She wasn't ready to deal with him yet. Maybe she never would be. She couldn't even tell if her speeding pulses were due to fear or to other emotions she feared naming.

"You never had time to run around then," Kalin said.

Casey steeled herself. Kalin had said plenty during the time they had dated about her habit of working almost every night. He was about to discover that some habits never changed. As for her plans for a simpler life, managing Cap'n Bob's would be a far lesser headache than the big French restaurant she had managed in New York, no matter how bad off it might be.

With Kalin present, Casey and Bonnie talked only of the changes in Winnie and gossiped about the various members of their high school class. Kalin contributed occasionally, but mostly he sat watching Casey's animated face as she described the various hilarious incidents befalling a student in culinary school.

She turned her head to beam her most impersonal smile in Kalin's direction. "Remember that moon watch you gave me for Christmas five years ago?"

Kalin's eyes were riveted on her face. "Yes."

"Well, I really loved that watch, but I hadn't been there three months before it died an unnatural death in a stock pot when we were learning to make *pot-au-feu*." She pulled back her sleeve and showed Bonnie her watch. "Now I buy ten-dollar watches that I don't mind losing. I can't count the amount of jewelry that went into the various culinary masterpieces we created."

Bonnie laughed and capped her story with a tale of what happened to the jewelry of beauticians.

Kalin stared at Casey with painful intensity.

All in all, Casey could only be glad when the lunch ended.

Kalin insisted on picking up the bill, even though both women protested that he had eaten nothing, and escorted them out to the parking lot.

Casey pointed to the rear of the building. "Look at that pickup of Joe's. I wonder where he got the money to buy it if the restaurant is in the kind of trouble I think it's in?"

"The payments are probably what put the restaurant in the hole," Kalin said.

Casey agreed and listed in her mind where she'd start that

afternoon. "That redfish we had was really tilapia. If the menu says redfish, what's on the menu had better be redfish, or there should be a reason given why it isn't."

"You've suddenly developed a militant look. Is this what you learned in cooking school?" Kalin watched her with delight.

"Cooking school merely developed my latent abilities. I was always the managing type, I'm afraid."

Bonnie started to laugh. "She was. Do you remember how she talked you into stealing a big chunk of that man from Beaumont's rice contest entry?"

"I'll never forget it as long as I live," Kalin said, grinning. "I found out later he was a karate teacher. If I had known that when he was holding me by the collar . . . "

"Is he really?" Casey asked, diverted enough to look directly at Kalin. "Well, I'll be. Is he still cooking?"

"He won Grand Champion again last year," Kalin said. "You know, Casey, if you enter this year, you could beat him. He's been Grand or Reserve Champion five years in a row."

Casey savored the temptation, but said regretfully, "I'm sure I'd be disqualified, now that I'm a professional chef. That man had to be a genius to come up with that bombe."

"He always wins or places in most of the other cooking contests around here," Kalin said. "Don't you think it's your duty to do something about it?"

Casey stared into space. "The newspaper did an article on his cheesecake baking years ago. I'll have to find it."

"Does this mean you're thinking about staying in Winnie?" Bonnie demanded.

"It depends on how Granny does." Casey turned toward her car. "I'd better get back to the hospital and tell her about the sermon. Come on, Bonnie. She'll love seeing you."

"I'll pick you up at seven tonight," Kalin said. "So don't say I didn't warn you."

Casey unlocked her car door. "I already told you, I can't go anywhere. I'm very busy right now, what with the LSAT and all."

Bonnie got in the passenger side of Casey's car, pretending she noticed nothing unusual.

"Then you'll just have to make time." Kalin prevented her from slamming the car door by placing his hand inside on the headrest. "I have a few things to discuss with you."

She avoided answering him by staring frostily at a spot on his left shoulder that appeared to fascinate her, waited until he removed his hand, then slammed the door, and started the car.

"See you tonight," Kalin said, and stepped back.

Bonnie said nothing until they were on the highway heading for the Winnie Medical Center. "He's liable to follow us to the hospital. He's determined to have his say, and if you want to know what I think—"

"I don't." Casey concentrated on the road.

"—you may as well hear what he has to say," Bonnie finished. "Where is he picking you up?"

"He isn't," Casey said. "I'm not going."

"Joe offered you a job," Bonnie guessed. "I figured as much. Give you a job, and you'll find a way to work yourself to death. And it's common knowledge Joe would like to get the heck out of this place and go on the rodeo circuit."

"He should. He's almost ruined Cap'n Bob's. It'll take everything I know to bring it back."

Bonnie rolled her eyes. "It sounds like a lifetime proposition to me. Maybe you ought to buy the place. You'd do a heck of a lot better with it than Joe."

Casey tried to look as though the idea hadn't already occurred to her. She had enough problems right now, what with trying to rest up and simplify her life.

This was all Kalin's fault. She needed a job as an excuse to avoid him, and if she wound up buying her own restaurant, she could blame that on him, too.

She stopped at the main stoplight in town and glanced at Bonnie. The satisfied expression on Bonnie's face told its own story, and Casey wondered if she was really that transparent.

She hadn't been home a day, and already she was making plans to stay.

*

Casey spent the afternoon delegating tasks and stirring the Cap'n Bob's staff into action.

She perched on a stepladder, scrubbing down the Louisiana bayou mural with paper towels and a bottle of cleaning spray. She wore old jeans and a red sweatshirt, and her hair was pulled back in a ponytail, from which several locks escaped.

Cap'n Bob's was noticeably thin of customers, so Casey put the employees to work doing small cleaning chores. The two waitresses applied cleaner to the windows, and the cook scraped his grill as if a Marine drill sergeant stood over him.

Joe Kerns was invisible, as Casey had shown the kindness not to hand him a bottle of cleaner. She had, however, looked around his office critically and suggested that he sort through his newspapers, as one or two of them looked like throwaways.

"It's seven o'clock, Casey Gray, and you're through here for the evening," Kalin said.

Casey, unaware of his approach, started violently and felt the stepladder rock beneath her feet. The next moment she was lifted off it by two strong hands that closed around her waist like clamps.

"On the contrary," she returned, glaring as well as she could with her hands full of paper towels and cleaner and her feet dangling at least a foot off the floor. "I've just gotten started."

Kalin set her down and took the spray and towels out of her hands. He deposited them on a nearby table.

"You have to eat, and I'd be willing to bet you haven't had a bite since lunch," he said. "Get your coat."

He wore dark slacks, a camel sport jacket, and a red tie—indications of his plans for the evening.

Casey backed off. He looked masculine and determined, besides making her feel weak simply by being Kalin.

"I'm not going anywhere."

"Are you sure you want to have this conversation here? With all the help standing around listening?"

"Why not? Call it chapter two in the ongoing saga. What's a little five-year delay?"

Casey wondered if she had flipped out. After all her resolve never to mention their public breakup again, here she stood, dredging it up and issuing a direct challenge.

He smiled at her. "You can either walk out with me like a lady, or you can get hauled out like the little heifer you are. Your choice."

When Kalin smiled like that, he meant exactly what he said. Casey wouldn't put it past him to haul her out over his shoulder. And she was hungry, she reminded herself.

"All right. Let me get my jacket."

She wasn't surprised when he walked with her to the desk where she had stashed her coat. She went to the kitchen window and told the cook she would be back in an hour.

"It will be more like two or three hours," Kalin said over her shoulder.

Casey decided to save her energy for the ordeal ahead. No doubt Kalin would love for her to contradict him in front of the employees.

"That's right. Throw your weight around," she said in acid tones.

"I gave you fair warning." He shoved open the doors and guided her into the cool, damp darkness of the evening.

The only light in the dark parking lot came from the two bulbs over the entrance to Cap'n Bob's. The two large arc lights that were supposed to light the parking lot needed replacing. Casey made a mental note of that fact.

"Stop thinking about this stupid restaurant." Kalin opened the door of his SUV for her. "Tonight, you're going to think about me for a change."

She held on to her temper with supreme difficulty. This was not a moment to let him know she was inches away from screaming at him. "All right, Kalin. What do you want to say that you haven't already said?"

The overhead light in Kalin's SUV illuminated his face, and he held her fixed with his steady, outdoorsman's gaze.

"Apparently I'd better say it all again," he said with quiet determination. "I don't think any of it took."

Casey braced herself. Kalin McBryde was the type of man who liked to be sure you thoroughly understood his position. Maybe he wanted to be certain she knew where she stood in his estimation.

Too bad she no longer cared to know.

"Oh, it took all right. You don't see me casting myself at your feet, do you?" She gave him her best glare. "You know what Granny always said: 'Don't trouble trouble, when trouble's not troubling you.'"

At that, Kalin smiled. "Are you saying you're trouble?"

"Are you sure you want to find out?"

"Sit down, Casey."

"I'm sure you'll understand when I say I'd rather not."

"Sit down, Casey." He moved closer, crowding her back against the seat. "You don't want me to steal a kiss, do you?"

She sat, fuming.

"And if you'd like to try casting yourself at my feet, I'm prepared," he added in suggestive tones.

She gathered herself to rise. "Don't hold your breath."

Kalin placed a hand on her shoulder. "Would it help if I cast myself at *your* feet?"

"Don't you dare," she yelled.

It was too late. Kalin dropped to his knees on the shell-covered parking lot and assumed the pose of a young man presenting his beloved with an engagement ring.

"Oh, gorgeous female—ouch. Try to restrain your passion until I finish. Please deign to spend a few moments in my company and allow me to spend a few dollars of my hard-earned money buying you dinner—ouch. Casey Gray, if you kick me one more time, I'll steal more than a kiss."

"Then get up from there." She grasped a handful of his crisp dark hair and tugged. "How did you know I was here?"

"Trade secret." Kalin rose and pretended to favor his leg where she'd kicked him.

"You called Bonnie," she accused. "The traitor."

"I'm going to shut the door and come around." He grinned at her. "Perhaps I should warn you that any movement on your part to escape will be met with my famous flying tackle."

This triggered memories of playing football with Kalin and being tumbled to the thick grass beneath him, where he held her still and kissed her. She closed her eyes.

Kalin slid in beside her and shut his own door. The overhead light went off, and Casey counted her blessings. At least she didn't have to face him in the light.

"What is it you want to talk about?"

"Don't rush me," Kalin said.

She heard the smile in his voice. "Do you mind if I take a nap while you prepare?"

"Surely I'm not that boring." He paused. "Let me begin with a question. What is it I said five years ago that makes you think you can no longer look me in the eye?"

She winced inwardly. "I didn't know I couldn't."

"Don't lie to me, Casey. It's on a par with those neutral little cards and notes I've gotten from you for the last five years. You hope I'll be satisfied and go away and leave you alone. How does it feel to find out I'm still on your case?"

"Awful. I can't begin to describe it."

Kalin chuckled. He laid one arm along the back of the seat and tugged a lock of her hair that had escaped her ponytail. "Look, I've already told you how sorry I am about all that nonsense I said to you five years ago. Maybe it will help if I also tell you it didn't take me long to learn that a man is damned lucky if he finds a woman who responds to him physically the way you did to me."

"I won't ask where you learned that." Casey wondered if it was possible for her face to glow in the dark.

"Good." Kalin chuckled once more. "I'd hate to have to tell you." His voice grew serious. "I was already ashamed of the way I'd treated you when you begged me not to break off our relationship. There were other ways I could have handled it without losing my temper in public and deliberately saying things I knew would hurt you. Believe it or not, I don't like my memories of that time any better than you like yours."

She believed that. Kalin had never liked hurting people and was always quick to apologize if he thought he had.

"What I also don't like," he continued inexorably, "is that you obviously still have trouble dealing with those memories."

Casey twisted her hands together in her lap. Kalin would sit there all night if necessary, until he felt satisfied.

"Well, it isn't easy for me to come home knowing that everyone in town remembered what a wonderful scene I'd created. I figured Merrick's party would give us both a chance to get it behind us." Her voice took on an aggrieved tone. "But instead of behaving with restraint and dignity, you had to make a show of dragging me off to dance in the dark."

Kalin broke into laughter. "As you may recall, restraint and dignity have never been on my list of virtues."

"I know," she grumbled. "So now that you've given everyone in town something good to talk about, how about backing off?"

"What is it you think I'm up to, darling? Are you afraid I want to take up where I left off five years ago?"

"After all that? No way." She sought for the door handle.

Sitting with him in the cozy darkness of his car with the odor of his favorite woodsy cologne teasing her senses and the warmth of his body all too close was not the way she'd have chosen to conduct a rational discussion.

Even his profile, silhouetted by headlights when a car passed by on the highway made her feel suffocated. Her heart began a strange, new rhythm, and she felt almost drunk.

Which she probably was, she reflected with inward humor. Kalin had always gone directly to her head.

"Let go of that handle. I'm taking you to dinner, remember?"

"Hope never dies. You might have changed your mind."

"Sorry." He sounded anything but. "This is going to take a lot longer than I thought. Is Galveston okay with you?"

"Galveston?"

"For dinner. You used to love going to Galveston."

"I don't care." That was a laugh and a half.

"You'll care fast enough if I take you someplace where the service or the food isn't up to par." He urged her to buckle her seat belt. "Sit back and rest, Casey. You still look like the last time you slept was about a year ago."

Casey found herself happy to relax a little. She watched the dark horizon on the drive toward the beach, practiced her deep-breathing exercise, and told herself she could handle it.

Kalin kept her entertained with a flow of talk about the sale of his book, which warmed her heart and made her smile.

"When the call came, I was in the shower, so I stalked to the phone stark naked and stood there dripping water all over the carpet. I'd figured it was some idiot wanting me to come get him out of jail for drunk driving."

Casey caught her breath and quivered at the disturbing thought of Kalin's naked body.

"It took me a moment to realize it was an editor. After I'd hung up, I stayed, drip-drying, jumping up and down, and calling all my relatives to tell them I'd sold a book. By the time I was through, I didn't need a towel."

Casey hoped he didn't know what he was doing to her.

He launched into a description of the revisions he'd been asked to make, several of which were things Casey had suggested years before, and asked if she was interested in accepting a position as manuscript critique artist.

They had arrived at the Bolivar ferry, and Kalin drove onto the boat at the direction of the deck hands.

"I'd never read a Western until I met you," she said. "Now I love them and keep up with all the latest."

"Good." Kalin parked his car and switched off the motor. "You have a better understanding of Westerns than most English professors I've met. Want to get out?"

Casey followed him to the rail and let the cool, damp wind flow over her face. As the ferry plowed through the bay toward Galveston Island, the wind grew cooler.

"Are you warm enough?" Kalin asked.

"This is balmy weather compared to what I'm used to."

He wrapped both arms around her and pulled her against him. "In that case, you can keep me warm, because I'm freezing."

He radiated warmth and comfort, and his arms made no demands, so she stood in the haven of his arms until the ferry docked. Oddly enough, she felt more comfortable in his presence. She didn't even jump when his arms went around her.

He helped her climb back into his SUV as they neared the landing. "I thought I'd give you a chance to get after Gaido's the way you got after Cap'n Bob's."

Casey smiled. "We recent graduates of cooking school are full of idealism."

She absorbed the Galveston night lights as they drove along Seawall Boulevard to Gaido's Restaurant. This near Christmas, the seawall seemed relatively deserted, but the resort atmosphere remained and Casey soaked it up. She had missed the Texas Gulf

Coast more than she thought.

When they arrived at the restaurant, Casey fled to the restroom. She pulled the rubber band out of her hair and fluffed it as well as she could with her fingers, but it was no use. The face looking back at her from the mirror seemed young and guileless, totally unlike the sophisticated image she had hoped to project around Kalin McBryde at all times.

So much for sophistication. She rejoined Kalin and followed the headwaiter to a table looking out over the darkened Gulf.

"What are you having?" Kalin watched her study the menu.

"Blackened redfish, what else? I'm going to see if they try to pull a fast one on me like Cap'n Bob's did."

"What's wrong with fried shrimp?"

"Is that what you're having?"

"I think so. Why are you looking at me like that?"

Casey considered. Kalin liked fried foods as well as he claimed his father had. If the laws of genetics ran as unfairly as ever, Kalin had inherited his father's propensity for maintaining his lean, muscular physique on a diet composed almost entirely of fried foods.

"Well?"

She lowered her gaze and studied the menu, amazed at how easily she could look Kalin in the face now. "Nothing."

"You can have some of my shrimp. How about a salad?"

Casey agreed, and sure enough he ordered a salad and asked for extra dressing, then ordered a dish of fried scallops on the side. She was hard put to regard the food with her usual zest, instead of reckoning the number of fat grams in each bite of food Kalin put in his mouth.

She watched with fascinated horror the things Kalin added to his baked potato when he suddenly burst out laughing.

"I've been waiting for you to say something. It's easy enough to see you're dying to ask me if I've had my cholesterol checked lately."

"Not me." She returned to her own plate.

"Casey."

She looked up to find his brilliant gaze on her face.

"You can lecture me as much as you like about my diet. I'll even listen. If you care to take over planning my meals . . . " His voice trailed off suggestively.

Casey forked up a bite of redfish and pretended she hadn't heard. She admired the glittering display of Waterford crystal displayed in lighted cases all around the restaurant.

He grinned at her. "Of course, I have a terrible tendency to eat whatever I can grab from fast food places. What I really need is a live-in cook."

"You can't afford one until you sell more books. You'd better watch yourself, Kalin McBryde. You deliberately ordered all that stuff."

He suddenly looked like a mischievous boy. "I couldn't resist. The minute I mentioned fried shrimp, you started calculating my chances of living to finish the meal. Don't worry about me. Uncle Jack has already been on my case. Besides, I don't smoke and my father did, which Uncle Jack says is probably saving me." He added two more slices of butter to his potato. "If you don't get busy on that fish, I won't let you take a few of these shrimp off my hands."

Casey had lost most of her appetite, but she worked diligently at her fish and tasted the shrimp Kalin transferred to her plate.

He studied her face. "My father smoked and drank way too much, if you want to know."

Casey glanced uncertainly at him and said nothing.

"In the year before he died, he did a lot of crazy things."

"As a result of his diet?" Casey concentrated on her food.

"As a result of less oxygen to his brain," Kalin said in dry tones. "Maybe you're wondering why I went to law school after I'd sworn I'd never go. Well, after he died, I discovered he had made some interesting financial investments. One of them was to pay my tuition in advance at the law school he wanted me to attend, with the stipulation that if I didn't attend, the money would revert to the school's alumni fund."

In his letters, Kalin had never mentioned his sudden decision to attend law school. "So you decided to go?"

Kalin's smile was wry. "At the time, it looked as though I needed a well-paying profession. Most of Dad's other investments were no good, to say the least. And unlike most young lawyers just starting out, I had his law library and a lot of contacts."

Casey nodded her agreement and pretended intense interest in removing a bone from her fish.

His blue gaze pinned her. "That was part of what was wrong with me five years ago, you know."

She looked up, startled.

"I was discovering that my father had lost most of his money in various schemes, both legal and illegal," Kalin went on. "The legal ones were women and race horses."

Casey looked at him in disbelief. "Your father?"

"Yes. My father. It was one hell of a shock, I can tell you, and I was getting very little sympathy from you."

Casey returned her attention to her fish.

"I'm not blaming you," Kalin said. "I couldn't tell you about it back then because I was still too shocked myself. I just want you to understand why I was such a basket case."

Casey nodded once more, totally at a loss. She remembered Kalin grumbling when she needed to bake refreshments for one of her grandmother's meetings rather than sit holding his hand in the front porch swing for several hours. At the time, she hadn't known why he'd wanted to spend so much time with her doing nothing but holding her, but since she enjoyed being held by Kalin, she hadn't complained.

Unfortunately, her job and the promises she had made to bake special deserts for her grandparents' social activities demanded some of her time and attention, and Kalin had been in no mood to understand her obligations.

"Now that I've told you my troubles with my father," Kalin said, smiling at her, "it's high time you told me about yours."

Chapter 5

Casey froze before his determined gaze. She looked down and mumbled, "There's nothing to tell. I never knew him."

"I have a feeling there's plenty you can tell." He reached across the table for her hand. "Another reason I was so angry was that you'd never told me about your father and mother yourself. It hurt that you had such a lack of trust in me."

Casey tried to twist her hand from his grasp. "If you want to know the truth, I didn't tell you because I was ashamed. It isn't everyone whose father goes to court to deny his paternity and gets upheld. So if you want to get technical, I don't even know who my father was."

"Come off it, Casey. Anyone can look at you and tell Derrick Davenport was your father. Those eyes alone—"

"That's not what the judge thought," Casey returned.

Kalin smiled at her, and his blue eyes seemed to glitter. "Darling, you know as well as I do judges and courts make mistakes. Sometimes they know the truth, but for other reasons, they decide against the claim. That's what happened in your father's case."

She flushed but maintained composure. "All Granny told me is that my mother was a star-struck teenager who capped off her constant rebellion by running off to California as soon as she was eighteen. She wanted to be an actress."

Casey knew her voice held a considerable amount of sarcastic bitterness, but Kalin's face betrayed only sympathetic interest.

"Rebellion?" he asked. "Did she refuse to do her chores?"

"And how," Casey said. "Granny didn't know what to do with her. No matter what punishments Granny came up with, my mother still did exactly as she pleased."

Kalin smiled. "Whereas you gave in and did your chores?"

"Yes." Casey tried again to pull her hand back.

He refused to let her go. "Your grandmother used to say you would end up like your mother if you didn't behave?"

Casey's hand jerked in his. The flush that stained her cheeks probably answered him. She returned swiftly to her story.

"How my mother met Derrick Davenport, no one knows. She did manage to get a few bit parts in some movies, so more than likely she met him at a party connected with one of them."

"He was known for his capacity for partying, wasn't he?" Kalin asked when Casey showed signs of winding down.

She shrugged and kept her eyes on her plate. "Somehow he managed to keep their affair quiet, because that was one of the reasons my mother's story wasn't believed when she got pregnant. He was able to say she tricked him by sneaking into his home one night."

"It does seem hard to believe that he managed to keep it quiet," Kalin said. "Derrick Davenport wasn't known for his restrained lifestyle."

"I've often wondered if he thought she was lying about her age. All the pictures I've seen of her look terribly young."

Kalin smiled. "That's probably it. If you had slept really well last night, you'd look about sixteen."

Casey cast him a glance akin to loathing. "Anyway, she got pregnant. Instead of coming back home in disgrace, she chose to try to get Derrick Davenport to marry her by begging him to come back to her in all the tabloids. When that didn't work, she took him to court. He cast doubt on her claims by pointing out that he'd never been seen in public with her. Also, she had been seen with several other men. What it amounted to was that his lawyers managed to make it look as though my mother had deliberately seduced my father for the money. The judge denied her claim, and Davenport started dating Megan Murphy and married her soon afterward."

"What about the DNA tests?" Kalin kept her hand in his. "They said you were undeniably Davenport's daughter."

"It didn't make a bit of difference. Granny claims he bribed the judge." She shrugged. "I think the judge also denied her claim because she had publicized it so vigorously. It looked as though all she wanted was the publicity and the money. In other words, everything was all her own fault."

"Out for what she could get," Kalin murmured, in parody of the words he'd said to Casey five years ago.

"Yes." Casey's voice shook.

He tightened his grip and leaned toward her. "Casey."

Their waiter arrived with suggestions for dessert.

Casey sighed with relief as Kalin let go of her hand. He'd get back to the subject in a moment, she knew, but she'd have herself under better control by then.

Picking up her fork, she attacked her fish in hopes he'd find it hard to maintain intensity while she ate.

For once, she'd mistaken her man.

"What happened when the judge denied the claim?" Kalin fixed her with his steady gaze.

Casey pretended great concern with the remains of her fish. "The story fizzled out, despite my mother's efforts to keep the tabloids excited. I was born in a Los Angeles charity hospital, and she died two days later. By that time Granny had arrived."

"Your grandmother wasn't there when you were born?"

"No. She arrived the next day. My mother hadn't wanted her to come." Casey stopped, then added, "The daily papers didn't even report my mother's death."

"The tabloids must have reported it," Kalin said, his tone hinting that he already knew they had.

With a sense of mild shock, Casey realized Kalin had researched the story. Why was she so surprised, when she of all people knew of his talent for research?

"They did," Casey said. "'Davenport Love-Child Orphaned' or 'Turned Over to Charity,' depending on how they looked at it.

Nothing they said made my father so much as call the hospital to see what became of me."

"Does that bother you?" Kalin asked.

"I suppose it does," Casey admitted.

"How did you feel about it when you were growing up?"

Casey flashed him a look of resentment. Law school had taught him the art of staying on top of a subject with questions.

"I didn't know who my father was until I was twelve and snooped into Granny's private box of letters and newspaper clippings. She had always evaded my questions about my father."

"And?"

"It didn't mean much to me at the time. Of course, I read everything I could about Derrick Davenport, including stories about the paternity suit filed by an unknown actress who later died. Granny tanned my bottom and warned me against talking about it, so I never told anyone except Bonnie. Also, Granny had told the reporters I died a few days after my birth. That's why we were never plagued with periodic interviews. Granny is a very believable woman."

Kalin smiled and nodded. "Why didn't you tell me? Don't you think I'd have believed you?" His eyes were steady on hers, as if he was determined to have an answer.

Casey flushed. "By then I wasn't telling anybody. I had grown up enough to realize what my mother had done. Besides, what would you have thought? That I had some ulterior motive for telling you? No, I suppose not. You thought that when I didn't tell you." Her fingers clenched on her fork. Now Kalin would know why she felt so ashamed for having begged him to come back to her.

"Casey," Kalin said softly. "You know better than that."

"Do I?" She put the fork down with a clatter.

Kalin's face was set in determined lines. "What did your mother do?"

She glanced up. "What do you mean?"

"It's obvious you've passed judgment on her. What have you convicted her of?"

"I don't know what you mean." She clasped her cold hands together in her lap.

But she did know, and the realization was enough to banish what was left of her appetite.

The waiter arrived bearing chocolate cake topped with pecans, and Casey gazed on it with a lackluster eye.

After a swift survey of her tense face, Kalin said gently, "Eat your cake. I'll shut up until you're done."

These words banished what was left of her appetite. She forked the cake into pieces and pretended to inspect its texture.

Kalin, who had ordered cheesecake, watched her. "Well? Do you think you can make one like it?"

"I can make a better one. They haven't done anything unusual here." She nibbled a bite and indicated his desert. "What would really drive people crazy is a dark chocolate cheesecake. I'll bet it would absolutely send you into orbit."

Kalin ate his cheesecake with enthusiasm. "I can't wait. Call me when it's ready."

"You're a terrible judge of food. If it's fried or full of butter and sour cream, you automatically think it's great."

Kalin grinned at her. "I can't believe I've missed hearing you tell me I'm a lousy judge of food."

"I'll bet." Casey forked apart the pecans that had been clustered on top of her cake slice.

"I have. Really. Did your grandmother warn you that I was likely to treat you as your father had treated your mother?"

Casey was so involved with tearing apart her cake that she answered automatically. "All the time." She examined the holes in the cake minutely. "She was absolutely certain you were out to get me pregnant. When she found out your dad was Walter McBryde, she hit the ceiling. If you hadn't come over that afternoon and questioned her about her

Civil War silver, she'd have forbidden me to see you again."

"My manly charm," Kalin said.

"Anyone who showed the proper interest in her silver couldn't be a wicked seducer. After you left, she said that it was obvious Jack Johnson had done a good job in raising you."

Kalin laughed. "Too bad I had to ruin her good opinion of me by studying up on that silver."

"Actually, she was impressed." Casey looked up from the mound of chocolate crumbs she had created. "She praised your research abilities and said you were going to go far."

"Provided no one killed me first."

Alice Gray's old silverware hailed from before the Civil War, according to family legend, and survived the war buried beside the back steps of her ancestors' home in Alabama. Kalin, interested in mentioning the silver pattern in one of his novels, had discovered it wasn't manufactured until 1870.

Casey joined him in laughter. "I'll admit I was surprised at your lack of foresight."

"I thought she'd be interested to know the truth."

"Not Granny. Give her a romantic lie any day."

"Eat that cake. Those pecans are innocent."

Casey made a face at him. She knew enough about Kalin to know he'd return to the subject of her parents as soon as the waiter removed their plates and set cups of steaming coffee before them.

"Your mother's name was Cynthia, wasn't it?" Kalin leaned back in his chair.

"You probably know more than I do. You're a much better researcher."

Kalin smiled, and his relentless gaze never left her face. "I don't have the advantage of being in your shoes. I can only tell you how I felt when I first learned of some of the things my father had done. I wished I could change my name for a while, there. One day I came down on poor Merrick like an avalanche—she'd been doing her usual number about her cousin, son of the great Walter McBryde. Lord, I nearly hit the ceiling." He shook his head, grinning. "Merrick thought I'd lost my mind."

She prayed he would forget the question. "She seems to have recovered. She mentioned your dad at least once last night."

"Well?" He sipped coffee and ignored that. "What did your mother do that was so bad?"

"Other than get pregnant out of wedlock and try to force the man to marry her?"

"Don't you think she might have loved Derrick Davenport? He was a very handsome fellow with a lot of presence and charm. He must have been, to get Megan Murphy to marry him."

Casey's face quivered. "Granny said my mother died because she lost the will to live, so I suppose she must have loved him."

"Is it so wrong to love someone enough to want to sleep with him?" Kalin leaned forward, holding her gaze. "If it hadn't been for your grandfather's vigilance and Uncle Jack's constant lectures about sexual responsibility, I'd have made love to you while you were underage. You'd have encouraged me, and you might have gotten pregnant. I'm sure that would have been worse than anything your mother did."

Casey pleated her napkin, remembering how she'd felt as though she needed his warmth more than anything in her life. But she hadn't turned eighteen until the week after Kalin broke off their relationship, and so long as she was underage, he had been careful not to go too far.

"What would you have done about it?" she asked.

Kalin chuckled. "I'd have married you in about two seconds," he said. "Your grandfather would have seen to that. He watched me like a hawk watches a chicken yard."

"You'd have married me anyway, wouldn't you? That's the difference between you and my father."

"There's another difference," Kalin noted. "I loved you. Derrick Davenport, by all accounts, loved his own image better than he ever loved anyone else. But don't give me credit for virtue," he added.

"I'm a lot more like my own father than I care to think. The first time I got mad at you, I'd have probably accused you of trapping me into marriage. Then I might have used that to win any fights we had. If you thought I was tough with words, my father was a world-class expert." He rubbed his forehead with one hand and sighed. "It's a sobering thought."

Casey went still, understanding what he was trying to tell her. It was a new thought to her—that Kalin shared certain characteristics with his father that he felt ashamed of. She smoothed out the creases she'd made in her napkin and remembered how his words had overridden hers, until she'd resorted to begging.

"In a way, it's a pity we never made love," she said. "It might have been worth it to see your father go into action to save you if I'd gotten pregnant."

He laughed and reached for her hand. "Be thankful. Neither of us would have ever been the same. I'd like to see a picture of your mother. I have a feeling old Derrick Davenport lost out on that deal."

Casey smiled back. "Who are you kidding? You've probably seen more of her pictures than I have."

"I'd like to see some taken by her family. Did his lawyers get in touch with you when Davenport died?"

Casey shook her head. "Granny wouldn't let me near the telephone or the mail for several months, just in case, but they never tried to contact us."

"Did it ever occur to you to file a claim on his estate?"

"I was only thirteen years old, and Granny said it was best to let sleeping dogs lie." Casey laughed. "Can you imagine the excitement around here if all that stuff about the long-lost Davenport love-child had come out back then?"

"Lord, yes. Your grandmother is a smart woman." He paused, and Casey knew he was marking her characteristic, sparkling gray eyes with their thick, curly lashes. "Derrick Davenport had no other children. You'd have been a seven-day wonder."

Casey shrugged. "I was a seven-day wonder when it did come out. I had reporters calling me from all over the country. The only good thing about it was that they lost interest in me when I flatly refused to sue the Davenport estate."

Kalin nodded. "In their eyes, that was tantamount to admitting Derrick Davenport wasn't really your father, even though your mother named you Casey Evelyn."

Casey flashed him a swift glance. Almost no one remembered, or knew, that Derrick Davenport's real name had been Evelyn Hubert Casey. So far, no reporter had paid attention to her name.

"I just hope they leave me alone." Casey scowled. "Surely the statute of limitations has run out by now."

"The statute of limitations on old scandals never runs out. You know that. If they ever run a close-up photograph of you, the entire world will realize you're Davenport's child. Not to mention that DNA testing carries a lot more weight in the courts now." He stopped once more and regarded her over the rim of his coffee cup. "You'd become much too important to spend time with an undistinguished fellow like me."

*

Casey awakened the following morning with the feeling that her entire world had gone upside down. For five years, she had nourished the feeling that she would never be able to look Kalin McBryde in the face again. And now she had discovered that they had something surprising in common.

Walter McBryde had been a celebrity in his own right. Because Kalin had spent almost all his vacation time in Winnie with Dr. Johnson, Casey had thought of Kalin more as Dr. Johnson's nephew than as Walter McBryde's heir—but she realized now that Kalin probably knew as much as she did about suffering unwelcome comparisons to a famous person. Walter's career had ensured that Kalin's life was compared to his father's in every small detail. Kalin had said little five years ago, but in retrospect, she realized the reason he probably spent so much time in Winnie was to escape that constant scrutiny.

Casey gathered that Walter McBryde's death had unearthed illegal tax shelters and even some outright criminal deals with drug runners. Kalin had passed over that, but Casey read enough between the lines to know that he'd been thoroughly shocked when he began to settle his father's estate.

Kalin's ideas on love and life had come from Jack Johnson rather than his own father.

Casey showered and dressed, thinking of Kalin. They were more alike than she'd realized. No wonder Kalin understood how she'd fought against being thought like her mother.

He'd even understood that she was still wary of him and had made no effort to do more than kiss her goodnight at her door when he took her back to Cap'n Bob's the night before, a light brush of his lips over hers. Casey considered it more a gesture for old times' sake rather than a real kiss.

Casey hadn't known whether to feel relieved or annoyed, especially when she recalled him saying he *had* loved her—which in her mind implied that he no longer did. In fact, she probably ought to be surprised that he had kissed her at all.

"You look like someone threw sand in your eyes," Alice Gray told her when she arrived at the hospital bearing the usual cardboard box.

"It must be the pollen." Casey set a bowl of Scotch-style oatmeal before her grandmother and poured cream and sugar on it.

"It's the middle of winter out there," Alice said. "That I *do* know. Christmas in two more days, they say. Did you see that young man last night?"

"What young man, Granny? Joe Kerns? I told you. He offered me a job, and I took it." She placed one of Alice's own silver spoons in her hand.

"Not him. The other one. The one you were so keen on before you left." Alice's sharp old eyes studied her granddaughter's carefully expressionless face.

"Kalin McBryde," Casey supplied. "Yes, I've seen him."

"Well?"

"Well, what? He's just an old friend, Granny."

Alice Gray snorted and took a bite of oatmeal. "Don't try to tell *me* that, young lady. There's only one reason I know of why you'd suddenly want to go to law school."

Casey grinned and sat on the chair beside her grandmother's bed. News traveled fast, even news that wasn't quite factual.

"Absolutely," she said. "If I can outdo Kalin McBryde in law school, my cup will be full."

"Don't be tiresome, Casey Gray. He visited me a year or two ago. Asked me all sorts of questions about Cynthia." She sniffed. "It was easy enough to see what was on *his* mind."

Casey laughed. "Is there something wrong with the oatmeal?"

"Just the way I like it, and well you know it," was all Alice said. "Then stop fussing and eat."

"Don't get smart with me, young lady. I'm still your elder, and there isn't a thing wrong with my mind. Are you going to marry him or not?"

"Granny, I haven't seen him in five years. Marriage is the farthest thing from my mind."

Alice Gray kept her attention on her oatmeal. "No doubt that's why you look like you cried all night."

Casey wisely kept her mouth shut, but before heading for Cap'n Bob's, she drove home and applied more makeup. As she stood before the bathroom mirror glaring at herself, the telephone rang.

"Casey," Merrick exclaimed. "I'm so glad I caught you. Listen, I know this is sudden, but if you want to get accepted this fall, the time to take the test is right now. I've got the application forms, and I'm coming over with them right away. You'll have to pay a late fee, but that's nothing."

In fact, Merrick was so persuasive and so determined to be helpful, Casey found herself filling out the forms meekly and writing out a check for the fee. Merrick took the forms and rushed off with them, to get things started at once.

Casey stood in the doorway watching Merrick drive away, grinning and shaking her head. Casey's lack of a regular college degree no longer seemed to matter to Merrick.

A delivery truck turned in the driveway and disgorged the ten large boxes Casey had packed with her worldly possessions when she closed out her New York apartment. She had them placed in her grandmother's bedroom out of sight until she could unpack them. There was no sense in giving anyone premature ideas about her remaining in Winnie—even if she did, by some miracle, pass the LSAT test.

No doubt she had gone crazy, going so far as to pay good money to take a test she would probably flunk, but somehow the pretense that she wanted to go to law school gave her more strength in facing Kalin. Just why she needed more strength to face him, she wasn't sure, but one thing was certain—the process would help keep her too busy to moon about Kalin.

Shrugging, Casey grabbed her purse. Perhaps her credits would prove acceptable to a law school somewhere. If she didn't look out, she was liable to find herself being addressed as "Counselor" instead of "Chef."

Before she could get to the door, the doorbell shrilled.

"What time did you get up?" Kalin demanded, when she opened the door to him. "You should be resting."

He wore jeans and a plaid flannel shirt, with a blue windbreaker. Casey had to look away to keep him from knowing how the bare sight of him affected her.

"I'm on the way in to Cap'n Bob's."

"Cap'n Bob's." His tone left no doubt as to his opinion. "Are you meeting someone for breakfast?"

"Nope. I'm taking over for Joe for a few days." In her opinion, he had no reason to sound so annoyed.

"You're what?"

"I still have a lot of feeling for the old place." Casey pulled the door shut behind her. "Joe was itching to get away, and when I showed up, it was the answer to his prayers."

"I'm going to give him an answer to his prayers he won't soon forget," Kalin said grimly.

Casey faced him, all too conscious of her own tendency to hark back in time to cool, sunny winter days when Kalin would show up on her porch after a hunting trip with his uncle. "No, you won't. I need a job, and Cap'n Bob's is a real challenge. Joe has let the place deteriorate. In fact, I'm really looking forward to walking in there this morning."

"I'll just bet you are. What I want to know is, when do you sleep?" Kalin frowned at her tailored wool suit and pale pink blouse. "Why did you tell Joe you'd run that miserable restaurant for him if you're so busy taking care of your grandmother?"

"Granny doesn't take up that much time. It's preparing for the LSAT test that's taking up my time."

"Just so long as you make time to have dinner with me tonight." He followed her off the porch and to her car.

"I'll be working," she said.

"No, you won't. If you don't take a break and get some rest, they'll be hauling you out on a stretcher." To her surprise, he climbed into her little car beside her and buckled his seat belt. "I'll ride in with you."

She drove swiftly to Cap'n Bob's and listened to Kalin's commentary on why she should take a day off and go fishing.

At Cap'n Bob's, the man Joe had hired to clean every morning before business unlocked the door for her.

"Nice to see you this morning, Miss Gray," he said. "What's this I hear about you going to law school?"

Kalin burst into laughter, and Casey elbowed him.

"Actually, I'm still in the application stage," she said. "I'm hoping to outperform one Kalin McBryde on the LSAT. If I can do that, my goal will be achieved and I can retire from law without ever actually attending law school."

"McBryde," the janitor said thoughtfully. "Wasn't his father the famous crooked lawyer—"

"His father was a criminal lawyer," Casey broke in hastily.

Beside her, Kalin appeared likely to choke on laughter.

"All criminal lawyers are crooked," the janitor said. "Take it from me. Crooks need lawyers who are crookeder than they are."

Kalin agreed with considerable enthusiasm. "Casey will be even more famous than Walter McBryde. She's twice as mean."

Casey started toward the kitchen. "In that case, I don't see why I have to darken the doors of a law school. They ought to grant me a license and let me hang out my shingle tomorrow."

"There's one thing you learn in law school that you can't learn anywhere else," Kalin said, grinning. "That alone is worth the entire price of the tuition."

"Oh, yeah?" Casey started toward the kitchen. "What is this wondrous item?"

"Legalese."

Chapter 6

Casey had to admit Kalin had a point. Soon after she arrived at Cap'n Bob's Cajun Cooking, she and Joe Kerns settled at a table with a thick sheaf of papers between them. Casey calculated it would take a good two years of law school before she could even decipher the first page of the legal document.

She wished Kalin had stayed, but he had borrowed her car to run an errand.

"Look, Joe," she said. "I'm not accustomed to making decisions this quickly. I'll need to consult a lawyer."

"It's a good thing you have one on tap, then, isn't it?" Joe said slyly. "It's just that I'd like to get this done as soon as possible. The sooner I can be shed of the restaurant, the sooner I can hit the rodeo circuit. I'd like to be able to tell Dad I sold it to you."

During her five years away, Casey had cherished a dream of returning home and opening a restaurant. She'd be able to live in the country, with her favorite work to do and a built-in, appreciative audience to sample her new recipes.

It hadn't taken Joe long to discern Casey's thoughts when she glanced around at the state Cap'n Bob's had fallen into.

"Right now, with Granny in the hospital, I don't know from one day to the next what my schedule will be," she said. "Restaurants take up a lot of time, you know."

"Tell me about it," Joe said bitterly.

Casey tried not to let her feelings show. Everywhere she looked problems called for her attention. She couldn't concentrate on Joe's business proposal when her training called for her to tackle the out-of-date foods in the freezer.

When Joe left, she methodically addressed one problem after another in the kitchen, then took refuge in Joe's office to recruit her forces before facing the next round of items Joe had let slide. While she rested, she drafted an advertisement she hoped would persuade people to give Cap'n Bob's another try.

"Is the world's greatest cook speaking to customers today, or is she in hiding?"

Casey, brooding over a photograph of Captain Bob Kerns that sat on the desk, glanced up. Kalin leaned against the doorframe with his arms folded across his chest, smiling at her.

She stared at him with new eyes. She had so armored herself against him, she forgot the way she had once looked at him, cataloging by item the various things she found attractive.

"If you don't stop looking at me like that, I'll have to come over there and kiss you." He pushed off the door.

Casey lowered her gaze at once, startled into confusion. How had she forgotten the strength of his arms and chest, hidden beneath the flannel shirt tucked neatly into the waistband of a pair of well-worn jeans?

She eyed the jeans appreciatively, remembering the feel of the old denim beneath her cheek, and the resilience of his thigh muscles beneath it. She hadn't thought deliberately on those things in five years and now she found it exhilarating.

The jeans moved, and seconds later Kalin knelt on the floor before her, looking up into her face. "Are you all right?"

"I'm fine, thank you." She looked back at him gravely, covering her confusion with politeness.

"You look better," he noted and took her hand. "Have you booted Joe out and taken over his office?"

"I don't know where Joe went. He dumped it all in my lap and ran, so I'm getting to do as I please." She smiled and indicated the ad she had drafted.

While he read it, she took in every detail of his profile, from the hawk's beak nose to the long, straight lashes.

He glanced up at her and she blushed scarlet, like a teenager caught reading erotica. His hands captured her face and held it tilted toward him. Now she found herself savoring his touch on her face and wishing he'd touch her all over.

Kalin stared at her. His long fingers trembled against her jawline. "I won't ask what you're thinking. Whatever it is, I'm sure I'd love to oblige you, but I brought my relatives here to eat and they're clamoring to see you." He kept his hands on her face while he stood and leaned down to kiss her nose lightly. "So come on out and socialize."

"Your relatives?" Casey squeaked in dismay. "Why didn't you wait until I've had time to straighten out the kitchen? I don't like the way these cooks are handling the shrimp Creole or the crawfish étouffée, and Joe has instituted some cost-cutting measures that are absolutely criminal." She leaped to her feet and shoved her hair back from her face. "I'd better get back there and see about it. Why did you have to do this to me?"

Kalin stepped back. "You aren't raising havoc in the kitchen right now. You're sitting down with us and testing out the cooking yourself."

"You're now on my enemy list, Kalin McBryde. Only someone bent upon malice would do this to an old friend. I was actually hoping no one important would show up until after Christmas."

Casey searched her purse wildly and finally succeeded in locating the hairnet she'd tucked in that morning. She shucked off her wool jacket and headed in a purposeful way for the door.

Kalin blocked her. "I resent being called an old friend."

"Old enemy?" She blinked at him, thinking of the kitchen.

"I'll let you know. In the meantime, forget the cost-cutting in the kitchen and come sit down with us. It's lunchtime, and I'd lay a bet you haven't eaten a thing this morning." He guided her out the door and into the dining room.

Casey, too shattered by his touch to react with her usual decision, meekly walked beside him toward a large table with three persons already seated at it, studying menus.

She recognized Dr. Johnson's wife, Annie, but the other two women were strangers to her.

"Mother, Lydia, I'd like you to meet Casey Gray, the new manager of Cap'n Bob's." Kalin kept one arm around Casey's shoulders as he pulled a chair out for her. "She claims she hasn't had time to straighten things out in the kitchen, so we can help her assess the food."

Stunned, Casey automatically extended her hand when Kalin introduced his mother, Elizabeth McBryde, whose beautifully cut mouth, azure blue eyes, and long, straight eyelashes she should have recognized at once.

Lydia McBryde, Kalin's sister, had the same long-lashed blue eyes and thick, dark brows that Kalin had, but judicious plucking had tamed her brows into arches that gave her face a lively expression. During the time Casey had dated Kalin, she had never met any of his relatives. According to Kalin, Walter McBryde was feuding with Dr. Jack Johnson, because Dr. Johnson had dared to tell him exactly what fate his bad habits would result in.

Casey shook her hand also and said something welcoming, even as she sought a way to get to the kitchen without seeming rude.

Kalin forestalled her by pushing a chair against her legs until she sat down on the edge of the chair. Then he sat beside her and extended an arm across the back of her chair.

Although she had been on duty less than a day, Casey had already made her presence felt. The waitress on duty set out glasses of water right away.

Casey glanced over her shoulder at the window into the kitchen. The cook chopped away at vegetables for salads, and a stockpot of Cap'n Bob's famous Seafood Gumbo simmered on the stove. Perhaps the food wouldn't be too far below the quality she preferred.

"Stop intimidating the cook," Kalin ordered. "It won't hurt you to be a consumer for once."

"You have to watch everything at all times." Casey looked meaningfully at their waitress.

The girl straightened and swallowed her chewing gum.

When the waitress had taken their orders and fled, Kalin laughed outright and his female relatives joined in.

"I can tell you've been throwing your weight around already," he said. "They're all afraid of you, including Joe."

"I wish," Casey muttered, her attention on the silverware, which she noticed had entirely too many spots on it.

She registered an intent to have the dishwasher checked and raised her eyes to see Elizabeth and Lydia McBryde watching her with fascination.

Lydia's gaze zipped between Casey's face and the silverware. "Is something wrong with the forks? You keep looking at them."

"The dishwasher must be acting up," Casey said. "I'd better call the repairman out this afternoon."

"Forget the dishwasher," Kalin ordered.

"I can't help it. Every time I turn around, something else needs correcting. I don't know what Joe has been doing the past few years, but it hasn't included taking care of business."

Lydia inspected her silverware. "How can you tell by looking at the forks that something is wrong with the dishwasher?"

"See those white spots on the handles? That means it isn't rinsing properly."

"Lydia, if you mean to encourage her, I'll send you out to eat in the car," Kalin said.

Lydia wrinkled her nose at him. "You and what army?"

"We all want to know, Kalin," Annie Johnson said. "Let an expert instruct us, for heaven's sake."

"She works all the time as it is," Kalin complained. "Even your husband thinks she's on her last leg. He's taking her fishing on his afternoon off. Christmas Eve, mind you."

"That bad, huh?" Lydia McBryde viewed Casey with even greater fascination. "Kitchens must be really interesting."

"She's just a workaholic," Kalin said.

Annie Johnson said placidly, "I hope your New York wardrobe included a down-filled parka, Casey. I've never been able to convince Jack that not everyone thinks sitting on a beach or a lake with a fishing pole in the middle of winter is relaxing."

Casey smiled. "I have a good coat. But I was actually hoping Dr. Johnson would remember it was Christmas Eve and forego the fishing trip."

Kalin and Lydia began to laugh.

"If you mean you hope we remind him, we wouldn't waste our collective breath," Annie said. "It's his afternoon off, and that means he will be fishing. He has several very sick patients just now, so he'll stay close enough that he can get back fast if he's needed."

"I warned Annie about marrying Jack," Elizabeth McBryde said. "She wouldn't admit I had a point until they left on their wedding trip in a four-wheel-drive vehicle loaded with fishing rods. Annie had never fished a day in her life."

Casey glanced at Annie Johnson—slim, dark, and as lovely as her sister, Elizabeth. They had been the cherished daughters of a famous Texas legislator. Annie had married a country doctor and faded from public view, while Elizabeth had married Walter McBryde and held a position at the forefront of Houston society.

"Kalin's just like him." Lydia shot a glance at Casey. "Uncle Jack started training him early."

"Mind your own business," Kalin returned. "Everyone knows people who fish stay sane and even-tempered, no matter what."

"Do you like to fish, Casey?" Lydia asked.

Casey smiled politely. "I used to, when I lived here. I was good at handling crab traps off the pier."

"She worked all the time then, too," Kalin interjected. "The only day I could take her fishing was Sunday, and her grandparents thought that was almost sacrilegious."

"You used to work here, didn't you?" Lydia continued. "Was it fun, being a cook?"

"Most of the time I enjoyed it, because I like to cook things for people. They discovered I had a talent for management while I was at the Culinary Institute, so I don't often work as a cook anymore unless I'm needed."

"Merrick was telling us you made some wonderful things for her party the other night," Elizabeth McBryde said. "She said you used ordinary ingredients Annie had on hand."

Casey nodded. "If you have milk, sugar, eggs, and flour, you can do plenty. Mrs. Johnson's kitchen is always well-stocked."

"Some years back, Kalin brought home a loaf of the most wonderful bread I've ever tasted," Elizabeth said. "You must have been a good cook even when you were quite young."

"Kalin says you like to cook the way he and Uncle Jack like to fish." Lydia seemed to find the idea enchanting. "Can you teach people to cook?"

"Lydia, please don't bug Casey about teaching you to cook," Kalin said. "Her grandmother is sick, and she's had this restaurant dumped on her, and she's probably going to try to work her grandparents' farm by herself. She needs a couple of hours to herself to sleep at night."

"She won't get those if you have anything to say about it," Lydia shot back. "Besides, I just thought she might need someone to help in the kitchen here. After all, I'm out of school now and I don't have a job yet."

Casey swallowed a sip of water the wrong way and coughed until Kalin patted her on the back.

Lydia was barely twenty-one and slated to be one of the Houston debutante circle, according to Merrick. Walter McBryde might have lost most of his money, but he hadn't left his family destitute enough to force his daughter to work in a kitchen.

"Oh, lord," Kalin said. "Look out, Cap'n Bob's."

"I can work at the front desk or something. You don't have to go to school to do that, do you?" She turned large, pleading blue eyes on Casey.

Casey wondered just how much money Walter McBryde had left. "Actually," she said cautiously, "I may be needing some extra help. The business at Cap'n Bob's is about to explode."

"When can I start?" Lydia looked thrilled and clasped her hands. "What will I be doing?"

"Probably after Christmas." Casey waited for Kalin or Elizabeth to raise objections.

Neither spoke. Elizabeth looked pleased. Kalin looked resigned.

Casey continued, "As to what you'll be doing, I'm not sure just yet. I'll probably start training you as an assistant chef."

"Assistant chef!" Lydia clearly thought this was the next best thing to head chef. "Can I come by tomorrow and see what goes on in the kitchen?"

Kalin groaned. "I didn't realize she was getting so bored."

"What do you know about it?" Lydia demanded. "The only thing you can find in a kitchen is the fish scaler."

"What else does one need to know?" Kalin grinned across the table at her. "I made the mistake once of offering to help Casey in the kitchen. Never again."

The waitress arrived with salads and coffee, and Casey ignored the interest this statement generated by inspecting the salad and tasting the coffee. Lydia watched her every move with the look of one beholding a master at work.

"What are you doing?" Kalin asked. "I told you to quit working and eat."

"Leave her alone, Kalin McBryde. I want to see what she does next." Lydia appeared to be waiting for Casey to fling the salad at the hapless waitress.

Casey took pity on her when the other three broke into delighted laughter. "I'm making sure the coffee is less than fifteen minutes old, and checking to see that the salad has been made with fresh lettuce and not that wilted stuff I told them to get rid of."

"Joe has let the quality suffer," Annie said tactfully.

"That's putting it mildly," Casey cast a malevolent glance toward the kitchen. "They haven't seen anything yet."

"You're intimidating the cook again," Kalin pointed out. "If you keep doing that, we may wind up with ptomaine."

"Not in any restaurant of mine." Casey shoved back her chair. "I'd better see what they're up to."

Kalin blocked her exit with an arm across her path. "I told you, you aren't going anywhere. Eat that salad, or you'll wear it."

There was a pregnant pause.

Elizabeth and Annie made a production of readying their napkins and picking up their forks.

Lydia sat on the edge of her chair.

Casey exchanged a long stare with Kalin. "I am not accustomed to being spoken to in that tone. I ought to call the cook and have him throw you out."

"The cook is probably afraid enough of you to try it," Kalin replied. "Why don't you save time and throw me out yourself?"

"I have too much dignity to get involved in altercations with paying customers," Casey said. "I'll have to think of something else that will compensate me for the mental anguish of remaining at this table with you."

"Maybe he should become a dishwasher," Lydia suggested.

"I had in mind something more like having him scrub out the garbage dumpster with a toothbrush."

Under the cover of the laughter this remark evoked, Kalin covered her hand with his own. "If I thought it would make you feel any better, I'd do it."

Casey pinned a resolute smile on her mouth. "I'll bake your family something special for Christmas." She attacked her salad.

Kalin regarded her steadily. "No, you won't. You're going to be resting."

"That *is* resting to me," Casey said.

"May I come watch while you bake it?" Lydia asked.

Lydia's pleading blue eyes, so like Kalin's, and her youthful enthusiasm were hard for Casey to resist. She nodded while Kalin objected and the two older women laughed indulgently and teased Lydia.

Lydia said cheekily, "If I want to catch a man, I'd better learn something about cooking. Look how Casey has poor old Kalin tied up in knots."

Casey flushed. "It's probably his new manuscript that has him tied up in knots. He never said much about my cooking." The salad suddenly tasted like paper, and she put down her fork.

Kalin watched her closely. "That was because the moment I said anything at all, you started trying to get me to comment on every little detail of the taste or texture." He shrugged and smiled. "Like me when you made a remark about one of my stories."

Casey recalled the way Kalin had worried over every detail of his plots or characters, and a small smile shaped her mouth. She'd soon learned not to comment unless she considered the matter serious.

She glanced up, saw all three women's interested gazes fixed on her, and colored again.

It was going to be a long lunch.

*

"You shouldn't encourage her," Kalin said when Casey opened her door to admit him and Lydia that evening. "She gets these enthusiasms."

Lydia's azure eyes sparkled. "How will I ever know what I want to do if I don't sample a few things?" she asked. "Casey, my mother and Aunt Annie want you to spend Christmas Eve with us. After all, a day spent fishing with Uncle Jack calls for a reward, and Aunt Annie says the least we can do is warm you up with egg nog."

Casey stepped aside so the pair could enter. "That's very kind of them, but I've planned to spend the evening with Granny at the hospital."

Lydia immediately said she understood, but Kalin, with a brown folder full of paper in his hands, studied her with suspicion. "I don't want you in this house alone on Christmas Eve."

"I won't be here. I'll be at the hospital." She ushered Lydia toward the kitchen. "You can pick her up about midnight. Or is that too late?"

"Since I'm going to be right here, you can keep her busy the entire night. Are you sure you aren't too tired for this?" He laid the folder on the coffee table and scanned her face.

Casey, who had spent the day at Cap'n Bob's supervising the dishwasher repairman and the professional cleaners she had hired, laughed. "Are you kidding? I'm dead on my feet after ordering people around all day. Now I'm about to relax. Is that a legal brief or a new Western novel from the future Louis L'Amour?"

"It's my new Western. I'll leave it for you to read in your spare five minutes before bed." He followed them to the kitchen and looked about at the ingredients and pans and bowls Casey had already placed on the table. "What is this spectacular dish you're going to create?"

"It's a creation called *Croquembouche*. It's shaped like a Christmas tree and made from cream puffs. You'll be able to eat off it for days."

Kalin had made no move to force their relationship toward a more intimate footing, and consequently, Casey felt comfortable in his presence. Knowing he had probably planned it that way didn't mitigate the effect.

"That big?" Kalin pulled out a chair at the kitchen table.

Casey watched the way his shoulder muscles bunched and elongated with the motion. "You'll be impressed," she promised, and forced her gaze to the big apron she handed Lydia.

"Are you going to let him sit there in the way and not do

anything to help?" Lydia demanded.

"Not a chance," Casey said. "Go watch TV, Kalin."

"Is there any coffee?" Kalin asked.

"I'll make some in a minute. We've got to get started on our cream puffs, so you'd better move it."

Kalin went, grumbling, and Casey heard him settle on the sofa with his manuscript and switch on the television.

Surprisingly, Lydia was a great help in the kitchen. She did everything Casey asked and had the good sense to wait for direction if she wasn't sure how to proceed. Casey was surprised at her eagerness to learn and found herself liking Lydia more and more, especially when the younger woman switched off her cell phone and stashed it in her purse.

"I don't want anyone disturbing me right now," she said. "This is too important."

Casey was stunned. One of her major duties at her old job had involved persuading the kitchen assistants to turn off their cell phones while in the kitchen.

"Is it true you're going to law school?" Lydia clearly found this incredible. "I mean, why be a lawyer when you can cook?"

Casey bit back a burst of laughter. "Good question. The truth is, everything is very preliminary right now. First, I have to pass the LSAT, but since Kalin promised to put on a wig and take it for me, I don't expect any trouble there. Then if I pass, I have to get admitted to an actual law school."

"Kalin promised to put on a wig?" Lydia repeated weakly.

"That's right, and I'm holding him to it."

Lydia looked toward the living room, then back at Casey. "Wait until I tell Mom."

"Don't tell her until after Kalin passes that test for me," Casey said, tongue firmly in cheek. "We don't want to remind him that kind of activity might be frowned on."

Lydia, grinning, agreed. "Mom will just say what she's been

saying for the past few years—that Kalin has it bad."

Casey refused to go there.

Between activities, however, she found excuses to peep into the living room where Kalin had his legs stretched out beneath the coffee table, reading through his manuscript. She liked seeing him there, in much the same position of five years before.

"Kalin said you never had a Christmas tree when you were little," Lydia said after Casey made yet another trip to the kitchen door. "He said your grandmother believed in the old Twelve Days. Are you going to celebrate them this year?"

Casey returned to the table and prepared to run another batch of dough puffs into the oven. "I haven't thought about it, I've been so busy. Granny's people were old Scottish folks who still celebrated Christmas on January sixth when Granny was little. I'll probably carry on the tradition."

"What will you do?"

"Old Christmas is like regular Christmas, but on January sixth. Some of the people didn't like it when the British Isles switched to the Gregorian calendar in the eighteenth century, and when they moved to America, they still refused to switch."

"So it's an old tradition?"

"It tends to be confined to country folks descended from Scotch and English settlers." Casey took up her pastry bag again and began squeezing out more dough puffs. "I used to keep careful track of the weather on the Twelve Days, so I'd know what the weather for the year would be. Then I'd spend the night in the barn on Old Christmas Eve with the animals and check Grandpa's fig trees. I'm not so sure the old Twelve Days isn't more fun than a regular Christmas."

"Kalin said he gave you twelve Christmas presents, one for each of the Twelve Days." Lydia grinned. "I think I'd prefer that myself. What's all this about the weather and the animals? He never said anything about that."

"Each of the Twelve Days between Christmas Day and Old

Christmas represents a month of the year, according to Granny. Whatever the weather is on each of the Twelve Days is an indicator of the weather you'll have during the corresponding month of the coming year."

"I've never heard of that." Lydia peered in the oven window at the expanding puffs. "What about the animals?"

"Old Christmas Eve is supposed to have powerful effects on animals and plants. At the hour of midnight, horses and cattle rise to their knees, roosters crow, elder bushes bloom, and fig trees bud, even if they're covered with ice. That's why I spent the night in the barn. I hoped to catch the animals in the act."

Lydia looked fascinated. "Did you ever catch them?"

Casey smiled wryly. "I always fell asleep."

She remembered the feel of Kalin's hands on her body as they lay together on a quilt atop a pile of hay in the old barn. That year she hadn't fallen asleep. She had simply been incapable of noticing any activity less than an earthquake.

Lydia sighed. "It sounds like so much fun, growing up in the country. Kalin told us how he loved to sit in the kitchen and write while you baked. No wonder he hasn't been human for the past five years."

Casey caught a movement and glanced toward the door. "If I were you, I'd have used him for crab bait by now."

Lydia laughed. "They do say like calls to like. He'd have attracted every crab in the Gulf."

Kalin growled and lunged for his sister, who shrieked with laughter and dodged behind the table.

From the safety of the table, Lydia cried, "If you have any compassion for mothers and sisters, Casey, you'll put him out of his misery and marry him tomorrow."

Chapter 7

Kalin arrived at Casey's house early Wednesday morning, with the trailer holding Dr. Johnson's bass boat attached to his SUV.

Casey opened the door to him with an exaggerated scowl, having expected something of the sort. "Where's Dr. Johnson?"

"Old Mr. Givens took a turn for the worse late last night. Uncle Jack was with him all night, and this morning he was called out early because Bobby Frye broke a vase and stepped on a piece of the glass. Uncle Jack is sewing up his foot as we speak."

"In that case—"

"Forget it. He said you were the severest case of a person in need of a fishing trip as he's ever seen." Kalin grinned at her. "So get a move on. If we don't get on the lake, we'll miss the best fishing."

Casey glowered at the sky. She wore jeans, an ancient sweatshirt, an old car coat, a sock hat, and she carried a pair of fur-lined gloves. "It looks like rain."

Kalin glanced at the lead-colored sky. "So?"

"If I get soaked, I'll have to kill you."

"What's a little rain? Come on. The fish are waiting." He hauled her out the door. "Stop stalling."

"I'm not sure I care to eat anything dumb enough to let itself get caught on a day like this."

"I'll eat it," Kalin said. "Fried."

Kalin helped her into his vehicle and drove to a private lake located in the far reaches of the rice fields. Several hundred ducks rose into the air and vanished upon their arrival, and hawks perched at intervals in the trees that grew on the levees bordering the rice fields. These sights had been familiar to Casey since her childhood, and she loved them.

Kalin backed the trailer down toward the water. "Guess who gets to help me launch the boat."

"My favorite activity, next to sitting in a duck blind."

Kalin laughed. "You were pretty miserable, weren't you? Misery is part of the fun of duck hunting."

"No, thanks. Give me a fire, a fresh cup of coffee, and a new cookbook any time."

She leaped down without assistance and helped him lower the boat into the water and release it. She settled on the comfortable seat and watched Kalin start the motor and guide the boat toward a small cove. He killed the motor before they reached the cove and used a paddle to steer them toward it.

When they drifted to a halt, she took the baited pole Kalin handed her and balanced it in her gloved hands, letting it rest on the rim of the boat.

"You're supposed to sit up and pay attention to that cork," Kalin said, smiling at her.

She glanced away casually. Things had changed between them again, and Casey was unsure how to behave. She only knew she mustn't let Kalin see how his smile affected her. Or that she noticed the fact that she was alone with him in a boat on an otherwise deserted lake.

Once upon a time, they'd have found a secluded cove and made use of their aloneness. But Kalin was rigging up a fly, which meant he intended to wear himself out casting it. So much for resurrecting old times.

"I thought the object of this trip was to get me to relax," she pointed out. "If I have to watch a cork, I'll get all tense and nervous every time I see it bobble."

"If you see it bobble, just pull it up," he said.

Casey muttered a comment about the state of her nerves and settled back. Every now and then, the boat rocked slightly as Kalin cast his line, but she found it surprisingly easy to let her mind drift.

She gazed at the level horizon beyond the lake. Although leafless tallow trees bordered the lake, the flat Texas coastal plain stretched in all directions, with the only hills provided by rice field levees. She loved the sight.

Watching Kalin from beneath her lashes, she wondered if she could outlast him in impersonal, friendly behavior. Last night, after she and Lydia had completed work, he kissed her swiftly one time at the door and left.

Good, she told herself. What if she let herself fall for him again and he rejected her a second time? And just how badly did he think he had damaged her self-esteem that he had to keep coming around until he was sure he had repaired it?

The fishing pole almost leaped out of her hands.

"You've got a bite," Kalin shouted.

Casey grabbed her end of the pole and jerked with all her might. A large bass flopped down on top of her feet.

Kalin stared in disbelief. "You landed him."

Remembering how Dr. Johnson and Kalin played with their lines and coaxed a fish toward the boat so they could net it, Casey had to laugh. "So long as I don't have to unhook it."

Kalin grinned at her. "More than happy to oblige. He'll taste great fried up in Aunt Annie's special corn meal batter."

"How do you know that fish isn't a lady?"

Kalin expertly unhooked the bass and attached it to a fish stringer, which he dangled in the water. "I thought sexing fish was an area cooks excelled in."

"Not me. I developed the flu when we worked on fish."

"I'll bet you developed pneumonia when you studied the fine art of duck cookery."

Recalling the way Kalin had stood over her, lecturing her forcefully on how to dress a duck, Casey had to laugh. "You're right. A very severe case."

He baited her hook again and watched her throw the hook

back out in the water. She mentally adjured the cricket on the other end of the line not to attract anything.

But the fish seemed starved for crickets. Every time Casey sat back, her cork bobbled, wobbled, or just flat got sucked beneath the surface. By the time she had been forced to "play" two bass, she was heartily fed up with fishing as a form of relaxation. "Why don't you take this pole and let me have the fly rod?" she said.

Kalin, engaged in attaching a perch to the stringer, laughed. "Are you saying you aren't having a good time? You don't know it, but this is good for you. Throw that line back out."

Casey grumbled and threw the line back out. Once more Kalin watched her.

"I don't like the way you're throwing that line," he said. "You act like you hope nothing bites."

Casey cast him a speaking look.

"Get busy and fish," he said, laughing.

She settled back once more to watch Kalin, a man who fished for the love of fishing. She studied the way his arms and broad shoulders moved as he cast his fly and played it over the water. No wonder he stayed in such good shape, with all that upper-body exercise.

The tip of her pole bent toward the water, and her cork went invisible. Annoyed at the interruption, Casey jerked back hard on the pole. She had hooked a bream, and its broad, flat body smacked Kalin on the side of his head as it flew into the boat.

Kalin dropped his pole. "Are we now catching flying fish?"

"I thought it was another bass. You have to put a lot of power into landing a bass, you know."

"You almost landed him on the other side of the boat."

"I knew thoughts of how he'd taste fried would keep you from letting that happen."

The fish flopped on the bottom of the boat. While Kalin removed the fish from her hook, Casey searched the bait bucket for the biggest, fattest cricket available.

She found a dried elm leaf, which served the purpose admirably. It resembled a cricket, once she threaded the hook through it several times, and Kalin watched as she threw her line back out without saying a word.

She closed her eyes. If anything sampled that elm leaf, it deserved to be caught and eaten.

Her mind returned with the tenacity of a compass needle to Kalin. Once he'd satisfied himself that she was back to normal, he would probably fade from her life. She could not afford to let herself become dependent on him for happiness.

Casey frowned. How could she go about convincing him that she was in fine shape? She had the restaurant and her grandmother. She did not need him.

"Casey."

She opened her eyes, startled.

"You're supposed to watch that cork."

She cast a stunned glance toward the red and white bobber. It rested placidly on the water, rocking gently with the breeze.

"I knew there was something funny about that last cricket." Kalin reached for her pole.

Casey held him off with her foot. "Mind your own pole."

He wrestled her for possession of the pole and hauled in her artfully attached elm leaf. "Something tells me you don't have the proper attitude toward fishing."

"I could have told you that myself."

"Another word out of you, and I'll report you to Uncle Jack. Cases like yours, he usually refers to a shrink."

"That might not be a bad idea. I could get analyzed and have someone explain to me why I'm out here letting you bully me. Give me your pole. How can I relax if fish keep bothering me?"

"If I gave you my pole, you'd drown my fly." Kalin baited the hook with a cricket. "Besides, I'm counting on your skill to provide me with a fried fish supper."

"Kalin."

"Yes, darling?"

He kept calling her darling, but he was nothing more than an old friend, she reminded herself. "It's Christmas Eve. Mrs. Johnson always serves egg nog and fruitcake on Christmas Eve. You told me so yourself."

"Want to come join us?"

"I'm sitting with Granny." She thought of the way Alice had tried to forbid her to spend Christmas Eve at the hospital when there was a perfectly good celebration going on at Dr. Johnson's house. "I was just reminding you of what you're missing."

Kalin glanced up at her from beneath his long lashes. His brilliant eyes took in her smile. "They'll save me some." He supervised the return of her line to the water, then went back to casting his fly.

"Kalin."

He caught his fly and turned to look at her.

"I felt a drop of rain."

"It won't rain. I forbid it."

But the weather ignored him. The sky grew steadily more overcast, and the drops began to fall in closer succession, until even Kalin had to admit that it was raining.

"I hate to leave when you're doing so well." He unhooked yet another fish for her, a perch this time.

"I'm not doing well." Casey huddled in her car coat and wondered how soon she'd start to feel the wetness seeping through. "The fish are just hungry for crickets, that's all."

Kalin grinned at the miserable picture she presented. "I can see you're a fair-weather fisherman. We'd better head for the car. It looks like it's building for a real downpour."

"That's what I've been trying to tell you."

By the time he headed the boat toward the car, the rain fell in earnest. When she helped reload the boat on its trailer, Casey felt the rain soaking her shoulders. She was nicely wet by the time Kalin drove back down the isolated, dirt road.

"Are you all right?" Kalin glanced at her with concern.

The thorough wetting didn't seem to bother him at all, Casey noted with resentment. "I'm dreaming about a hot shower and a hot cup of coffee."

He grinned. "Good. So am I. What's the fun of a fishing trip without a little misery?"

Casey rolled her eyes. He didn't want to hear her comment on that remark.

By the time they pulled up in the driveway at her house, she shivered in earnest. Kalin had turned the heater up full blast.

"Inside with you," he said. "Get into the shower right away. I'm not having you come down with pneumonia."

Casey said something uncomplimentary about fishing as a form of relaxation and climbed stiffly down from the Cherokee while Kalin took her keys and unlocked the door.

She went into the bathroom, stripped off her damp clothing, and stood beneath the hot shower until she felt warm again. She wrapped herself in a thick towel and went to her bedroom—after first ascertaining that Kalin was busy in the kitchen—and dried her hair and put on her warmest robe.

"You're still cold." Kalin appeared in the doorway to her room and set a cup of hot coffee down on her bedside table. Then he took her in his arms.

Casey let him hold her and wondered what was coming next. His intense outdoorsman's gaze had taken her in from head to foot, and he didn't seem pleased with what he saw.

He sat her down on her bed, handed her the cup of coffee, and stood over her while she sipped it.

"You don't have a bit of natural resistance left," he said sternly. "Get into bed."

Casey climbed into bed, robe and all, surprised at her own lack of interest in arguing about all the things she had to do. Fishing, it seemed, really did relax a person in the end.

Kalin had shucked off his down jacket, and his flannel shirt beneath it was dry as a bone. His jeans were damp and he removed them without embarrassment and climbed into bed beside her.

She shivered when he drew her into his arms and tried to warm her with his own body.

"I don't think you have any extra fat on you anymore." He curled around her.

"I hope not. A fat cook is bad for business these days."

"I can see you have a whole new image brewing for Cap'n Bob's. I'll have to take my business to Dairy Queen."

"Oh, no you won't. Wait until you taste the new Cap'n Bob's cheesecake. It will make the foodie columns all over Texas, I promise you."

Kalin rubbed her arms vigorously. "I can't wait."

Casey began to feel warm and tingly as she sank beneath the spell of Kalin's warmth and his distinctive woodsy scent. "I have plans. Deep Dark Secret."

"Deep dark secret?" he repeated. "Is it the plans that are secret, or do you have some other secret you're keeping from me? I wish you wouldn't do that to me again. It was a very unpleasant shock to learn you were the daughter of a movie legend."

"I really don't know for sure who my father is." She yawned. "Deep Dark Secret is the new chocolate cheesecake that's going to make Cap'n Bob's famous all over the state of Texas."

He turned her to face him and pushed her hair back from her face. "I'll be your chief taste tester." He kissed her nose.

Kalin's attitude of old family friend had begun to grate on her, although she would have died rather than indicate it.

If Kalin could be friendly, so could she. "I'll start working on it next week."

Kalin chuckled. "Are you feeling warmer?"

"Yes, thank you."

"Yes, thank you," he repeated and laughed. The laugh sounded strangled. "You're enough to make a man swear off fishing."

"I wish."

"You might as well learn to love it."

"What for? When I get back to New York, fishing will be the farthest thing from my mind."

Kalin seemed to stiffen, although she couldn't be sure. He shifted so that her head lay on his shoulder.

"Are you going back to New York? After having all your things shipped home?" He hesitated, then added, "Your grandmother isn't likely to recover fully, you know."

He knew she had closed out her New York apartment. So did everyone else in town, she felt sure. The delivery people had probably talked.

"I know," Casey said. "She might go back with me."

That was a laugh. Alice Gray would no more leave Winnie for New York than open a house of ill-repute.

Kalin lay in silence a moment. He moved, and the next thing Casey knew, her head fell off his shoulder and he was leaning over her, staring down at her. His eyes, in the semi-darkness, were intensely blue. He appeared to arrive at a decision—and then took her face between his hands and kissed her.

He almost bruised her in his eagerness. He used his own tongue to open her mouth for his penetration then he filled her mouth as if he wanted to fill every bit of her at once.

Surprised, Casey automatically put her arms around his neck. Instantly he gentled, releasing some of the grinding pressure. Seconds later he lifted his head to look at her.

She stared back, unsure how to respond.

Kalin smiled. "I just want to kiss you. I didn't mean to hurt you."

Recalling a time when she welcomed the roughest kisses she

could get from Kalin, she closed her eyes. Now she had better fear her own response more than any roughness from him.

She could handle it, she told herself. Maybe she should not have put her arms around his neck.

Kalin leaned down and kissed her, coaxing her into parting her lips with the tender pressure of his own. She left her arms around his neck and let herself respond. This, she was prepared for, and she loved it.

He smiled at her. "I love to kiss you. Your lips are better than any cheesecake I ever tasted."

She smiled back. "This is high praise indeed."

"You have no idea." He kissed her eyelids. "Your eyes are so beautiful. I love to see them smiling at me." He touched his mouth to her temple. "I love to smell your hair. It reminds me of rich brocades. My grandmother had a closet of old clothes that smelled like your hair."

"Mothballs?" Casey asked.

Kalin chuckled. "Brocade. She put spices and flower petals in the closet with them. It was a wonderful smell." He ran his fingers into her thick chestnut hair and massaged her scalp gently. "Your hair even feels like those brocades."

Casey quivered. He was seducing her with words as well as with his touch, and either one alone had once been enough to make her beg him to love her.

She would never beg him again.

Kalin stroked his long fingers along her neck then followed them with his lips. Casey tilted her chin up. Air entered and left her lungs on a shivering sigh.

He kissed the tender area beneath her earlobe and his warm, rough tongue touched her skin. Her fingers dug into his shoulders before she forced them to release him. If she didn't get herself under better control, she would give herself away.

Kalin appeared to be enjoying himself. After all, they were in a bed together with no prospect of interruption—a situation they had only dreamed of in their younger days—and she offered no resistance to his lovemaking.

If she wasn't actively encouraging it the way she once had, maybe that was an improvement in his eyes. She even understood how she might have embarrassed him in those days, the way she moaned and used her movements to entice him.

He turned her head to the side to investigate her opposite ear, and shivers of pleasure raised goose bumps down that entire side of her body. Casey drew in a ragged breath and practiced her deep-breathing exercise.

She needed to focus her mind on something. Seeking desperately, she settled at last on the texture of Kalin's skin right there before her eyes. She studied it closely.

He lowered the zipper of her robe a few inches and transferred his attention to the hollow of her throat.

Once upon a time, Casey would have responded to this by shamelessly throwing her head back and lowering the zipper herself another twelve inches. Because she focused on his forehead, which was all she could see of his face at the moment, she was able to remain perfectly still.

Kalin lowered the zipper himself.

She caught her breath when she felt his warm lips at the pulse of her throat. She almost lost interest in investigating the evenness of his tan but caught herself swiftly when his intense gaze focused on her.

"Casey?"

"Yes?" She hoped she didn't sound as choked as she felt.

"What are you thinking?"

Wariness descended on her. "I was admiring your tan."

"Is that so? Is it dark enough for you?"

"It's just right. Perfect."

He kissed her throat. "Even enough for you?"

"Couldn't be better."

He kissed her lips, paying particular attention to the tender corners of her mouth. "Does it, then, meet with your approval?"

"Yes." The words came out on a gasp, because his hands brushed lightly across her breasts on their way down to clasp her waist.

"Good." He kissed her in earnest, using his tongue to probe deeply inside her mouth, and brushed his hands lightly across her breasts once more as he moved to massage her neck.

Casey tried not to lift toward his hands, but it was difficult, more difficult than forcing her arms to rest lightly around his neck as he kissed her. She tightened her muscles to restrain the shudder that threatened to give her away.

Kalin kept on kissing her. It was driving her crazy to allow him free access to her body without encouraging him to explore her further, but she managed it. She had never been one to lie passively while he kissed and caressed her, but if that was what he preferred, she could manage. Maybe.

He kissed his way down her neck and progressed into the valley between her breasts. His warm tongue covered the area with damp heat, then she felt the cool air bathe her skin as he lowered the zipper all the way to her waist.

This was the moment when she used to moan his name and dig her fingernails into his shoulders in her eagerness to feel his mouth on her. She practiced her deep breathing and waited, trying not to shiver with anticipation.

His hands touched her first, and she opened her eyes to find his enraptured gaze roving the area he had exposed. He used the pads of his thumbs to tease her nipples gently, and she bit back her gasp and tried to disguise the arching of her back.

The glittering, blue eyes met hers. "Would you rather I not do this?"

She stared at him, unable to speak. If he stopped, surely she would die.

He smiled at her and lowered his mouth to the tip of one

breast, and she caught her breath on a gasp.

The intense pleasure burst through her, roaring through her body and settling between her legs. Her control came perilously close to shattering as he teased the tip into hardness then transferred his attentions to the other. She shook, unable to stop the tremors, and flexed her fingers.

Kalin whispered something against her skin and lifted his head to kiss her lips as if he was deliberately trying to coax a response from her. She held on to her control, shuddering.

Inside, she flamed with the passion he aroused in her by simply existing. She had never bothered to hide or control it before, and she wondered if the effort might kill her.

Before, Kalin had behaved as if her passion drove his own. She thought she knew better now, but the knowledge did not bank the fires raging within her.

Kalin stroked his thumbs over her sensitized nipples and thrust his tongue fiercely into the recesses of her mouth.

And Casey's control broke. She moaned and writhed and arched, digging her nails into his shoulders in attempt to bring him closer still.

Kalin groaned and jerked her zipper back up so swiftly, it jammed. He turned her quickly on her side so that she faced away from him and wrapped her in his arms.

She was so caught up in her own anguish that she barely noticed that he sounded as if he'd just run a marathon, and that the arms that held her so tightly trembled.

She closed her eyes and lay still, wondering bitterly when she would ever learn.

"Whatever you're thinking, stop," Kalin said.

She said nothing. If she opened her mouth, she'd scream.

He kissed the sensitive area behind her ear. "I thought I'd have more control, but it's obvious I don't. When you finally responded, I almost went totally crazy."

Casey cleared her throat. "Is something wrong with that?"

"Yes, I think so," he said. "I can't help wanting to touch you and kiss you. You're the most powerful temptation known to man, to this man at least."

She turned her head to look at him then tried to sit up. He refused to let her.

"It's obvious enough that I hurt you a lot worse than I thought five years ago. You're still not over it. I can't make love to you until things are right between us."

"Things were right between us five years ago," she reminded him in dull tones. "You wouldn't make love to me then."

"You were underage. With Uncle Jack and your grandfather both telling me the awful consequences of making love to a minor, it's a wonder I was able to kiss you without having nightmares."

"Maybe things will never be right for us."

"That," Kalin said, "is entirely up to you."

Chapter 8

Casey drove to the hospital that evening still berating herself over her loss of control.

Kalin, after lying with her a few more minutes, had wasted no time in putting his damp jeans back on and leaving. He'd claimed he had to return his uncle's boat.

Casey watched him leave, well aware that Dr. Jack Johnson could not have cared less about what hour his boat was returned.

Now that Kalin knew she could still behave like her old self, he should be satisfied. He could go back to Houston secure in the knowledge he had done no permanent damage to his old girlfriend.

Was she easy, or what? A few kisses and touches, and five years' worth of resolve vanished inside of less than ten minutes.

When she walked into her grandmother's hospital room that evening, she had somehow schooled her face into its usual expression of bland tranquility.

"You look better already," Alice Gray observed from her propped-up position on the hospital bed. "Jack Johnson should have been a psychiatrist. Then he could charge for those fishing trips of his."

Casey smiled and unpacked the box she'd brought. "Didn't I tell you? Dr. Johnson couldn't take me after all. He sent Kalin."

"Jack's nephew?" Alice's old eyes surveyed Casey shrewdly. "You may have mentioned it. Although I doubt it."

"What do you mean, Granny?" Casey leaned down to kiss her grandmother's cheek. "Why should I hide it?"

"You tell me," Alice said. "Why aren't you with him right now? That's what I'd like to know."

"I'd rather be with you tonight, Granny. You're my family. Kalin is with his own family."

"Hummph," Alice said.

Casey thought of Kalin and his relatives in Dr. Johnson's big living room, sitting around the Christmas tree listening to the doctor read the Christmas story as recorded by St. Luke from his Bible.

Alice frowned at her. "I hope you don't mean to live with him without the benefit of marriage, young lady. I brought you up better than that."

"Kalin told me years ago he didn't believe in living together." Casey set out one of Alice's own china plates and arranged a small, tender steak on it. "So that's the least of your worries."

"Don't you believe it, Casey Gray. Young men nowadays don't know the meaning of honor and fidelity."

"You forget, Granny. Kalin grew up under Dr. Johnson's tutelage, and he does know. I'll tell you a secret." She smiled and winked as she placed the prettily arranged tray over Alice's lap. "It wasn't my idea to remain chaste and untouched five years ago. I tried everything I knew to get Kalin to make love to me, but he kept holding out until I was older."

"Humph," Alice said again, an unwilling smile tugging the unaffected corner of her mouth. "Now that you're older, you'd better find out why he's holding out now, hadn't you?"

Casey laughed. "I guess I had. Eat your dinner so we can have Christmas Eve together."

Alice watched Casey cut the steak into bite-sized pieces. "So he still cares for you, does he?"

Casey hesitated, then opted for telling the truth. "I don't think so, Granny. At least, not the way he used to."

After watching her expectantly a moment, Alice said, "You're right about one thing. If he doesn't know the meaning of decency and honor, it isn't because Jack Johnson didn't teach him."

"True, Granny."

Alice focused her attention on grasping her own antique silver fork. "Hopefully, he knows how to behave the way a gentleman should."

Casey wondered what on earth Alice was getting at.

"And just as hopefully," Alice added in sharp tones, "you remember what I taught you about forgiveness and forbearance."

"Yes, Granny."

"Although I don't have much hope of it. If you had, you'd have come home sooner."

Casey maintained her calm demeanor with an effort. Five years ago, she went to great lengths to keep her grandparents from knowing how deeply Kalin's defection had stricken her.

She smiled. "I didn't know you missed me so much, Granny."

"Mind your tongue, young lady. I don't like what that precious cooking school of yours has done to you. Why couldn't you have gotten a job in Houston? You could have lived here."

"The best job opportunities in my field are in places like New York." Casey knew better than to say more.

"Hummph." Alice stabbed a bite of steak. "What are you going to do about that young man?"

"Kalin? Anything between us was over years ago."

Casey's voice didn't carry the conviction she wanted, and Alice looked her over from the top of her chestnut head to her polished loafers.

"Try that on my rooster," Alice recommended. "Well, that's his lookout, but I can tell you this, Casey Gray. The two of you were good for each other. You had the determination and optimism he needed, and he gave you his imaginative outlook and showed you the beauty of nature. It's a rare gift when two people are able to give to each other like that. Don't throw it away lightly."

That was all Alice had to say on the subject, for which Casey was grateful. However, Alice had plenty to say on certain other subjects, and Casey soon discovered she'd rather discuss Kalin. Even the old-fashioned Christmas pudding served with a spring of holly didn't distract Alice.

Although Casey disliked hearing the things Alice had to say, she listened without protest, knowing Alice's words were prompted by the older woman's real love and concern for her granddaughter.

"When you reach my age," the old woman said in closing, looking sharply at Casey, "it's ridiculous to pussyfoot around the subject of death."

Casey unlocked the front door to the old farmhouse and thought about what Alice had said. She was concentrating so hard she didn't immediately notice the living room was occupied.

A splash of colored light caught her eyes and she looked up, startled, to see a childhood vision rising out of the formerly dark corner of the room, just where she had always imagined it.

A tall, light-dotted, glittering Christmas tree glowed like a thousand candles in the dark living room. For a moment, she stood and stared in disbelief, before she set her box on the floor and let her feet carry her toward the vision.

She gazed at the star on top that glowed serenely down on the entire room, and let her eyes drift down the tree. The real fir tree perfumed the air with its scent. The branches were full and fresh. The decorations consisted of cut-out ball ornaments, old-fashioned aluminum icicles, a few wooden ornaments, and a real bird's nest; all the things she had dreamed of one day putting on her own Christmas tree.

Even the colored lights, the outmoded large bulbs that never blinked but glowed with deep, steady, comforting splashes of color amid the overall glow, were just what she'd wanted.

At the bottom of the tree a white cloth flecked with bits of glitter picked up the glowing lights and reflected them back in tiny twinkles of colored brightness. Gaily wrapped packages waited, just the way she'd have placed them, on the tree skirt.

Casey dropped her purse on the floor and reached out to touch the tip of a branch, crushing it in her fingers. The fresh fir odor reached her nostrils a moment later, and she reaffirmed the tree's reality by tapping an ornament that had a Nativity scene inside it.

It rocked on the branch and held her spellbound.

All her thought processes shut down. It wasn't important how the tree had gotten there, in the spot she'd always wanted it. She touched the tree once more and sank down on the floor to sit cross-legged before it.

The packages beckoned, but Casey had no interest yet in reading the green and red cards attached to each one.

"Aren't you going to say anything?" a voice came from behind her.

Somehow she wasn't surprised to find she was not alone. "Thank you, Kalin," she replied, still touching the tree.

"I wanted to make you happy." He knelt on the floor behind her. "I didn't mean to make you cry."

"I'm not crying. It's just . . . it's the most beautiful tree I've ever seen. Prettier even than the one at Dr. Johnson's. I wish Granny could see it."

Kalin's arms went around her. He sat on the floor behind her and pulled her against him, fitting her snugly between his legs. "You can leave it up until she comes home."

"She says she isn't coming home." Casey's voice quivered. "Maybe I can take some pictures."

Kalin was silent a moment. "I'll take some for you." He kept one arm around her and used the other to tip her head back to rest on his shoulder. "Aren't you even going to threaten me with arrest for breaking and entering?"

"Maybe with entering, but surely not breaking. I expect you found the key Granny insists on hiding under the back steps." She swallowed and nestled her head in the hollow of his shoulder. "I'd have given you the key myself for this. It's so beautiful. I'll never be able to thank you."

"You've already thanked me. Don't you know that?" He pressed a kiss on the upper curve of her ear. "You used to wish so hard for a Christmas tree. Do you remember telling me all the things you'd put on it? You went into it in such detail I knew it was something that meant a lot to you." He tightened his hold.

Casey rubbed her forehead against his neck. "I never bought a tree for my apartment in New York."

"You have to start creating your own traditions sometime." Kalin reached for a package. "You get to open a Christmas Eve present tonight." He placed a long, slender box in her hands.

Casey handled it with wonder, turning it this way and that to let the Christmas lights reflect off the shiny, foil wrap. "What are all the others for?"

As her bemusement began to fade, her heart beat in a new rhythm that sent an intoxicating rush of anticipation roaring through her veins, and it felt full to the bursting point. How much was due to the feel of Kalin's warmth against her back and how much to the Christmas tree, she could not have said.

"The Twelve Days of Christmas, what else?" He nuzzled her ear and kissed her temple.

She counted the twelve remaining packages as well as she could in the half-light created by the colored Christmas lights. "Thank you, Kalin. I don't know what to say."

She swallowed hard, tugging half-heartedly at the ribbon on the small package. Suddenly her mind slipped into gear, and she recalled with relief the item she picked up on a whim in an airport gift shop the day she left New York.

"Wait a minute. I have something for you." She struggled out of his hold and got to her feet.

When she returned to the living room, Kalin sat on the sofa and had laid the small package on the coffee table. She held out the shoe-box-sized package she'd wrapped in red paper.

Kalin pulled her to the sofa beside him and placed the small package in her hands once more. "Open yours first."

She switched on the table lamp beside them and admired the package. It had been professionally wrapped in silver foil. Excitement, fear, and longing all warred within her, and she scarcely knew which would win out.

"Open it." Kalin nudged her hand gently.

She pried at the tape securing one end of the package, eventually pulling out a long, slim box, which in turn contained a jeweler's case.

"If this is a diamond bracelet . . . " She lifted the lid.

"My diamond bracelet days are long since over." He chuckled softly against her hair. "I'm a starving author now."

He took the case from her strangely reluctant hands and opened it, lifting out a watch.

She saw the half-circle at the top of the dial that contained either a sun or a moon, depending on the time of day, and her heart contracted with pleasure.

"Oh, Kalin, thank you. It's even prettier than my first one."

Kalin lifted her left wrist, kissed it, and fastened the watch on it. "I don't care if it falls in the étouffée. I want to see you wearing it."

She promised he would. "Open yours."

He made short work of the wrapping and extracted what looked like a mallard duck decoy.

"It's a telephone," Casey said, in case he missed that fact.

Kalin's expression remained bland. "I see that." He turned the duck upside down and examined it.

"It's a life-like replica of a male mallard."

"I can see it's a greenhead." Kalin carefully turned the entire sculpture in his hands. "Is this some sort of revenge for making you learn to dress ducks?"

"You don't like it," Casey said, hurt. "It even quacks instead of ringing."

He set the duck on the coffee table. "Come here. I'll show you how I like it." He pulled her against his side.

"You hate it." She shoved at him.

"I almost bought one myself last year." Kalin laughed and rubbed his nose against hers.

Casey concentrated on the eyes that smiled into hers. She put up a hand to touch his face and trace the broad band of black above one of those brilliant eyes.

"Kalin, I—" She broke off and let her fingers run off his brow and into his hair.

"Darling, you don't have to say anything. Don't cry."

She smiled. "Do you know, when I was in high school, I used to sit in class and fantasize about the way your hair felt, and the way your skin felt, and how you smelled when we were on a date as opposed to when you'd just returned from a two-day duck hunt."

Kalin interrupted by biting gently at her bottom lip. "Don't waste time fantasizing about it, darling. Here I am."

His chest moved with silent laughter as he nibbled at her lips. She closed her fingers in his hair and tugged.

"Stop laughing," she commanded.

"I smell very nice, don't I? You're the one who caught all the fish." He sniffed her neck. "Yep. Eau-de-bass."

"You're the one who handled them."

Choking with laughter, they mock-wrestled one another until Kalin trapped both Casey's wrists. He pinned them behind her. For a long moment, they stared, gray eyes into blue, then Kalin reached for the lamp switch. The room fell into darkness except for the multi-colored lights on the Christmas tree.

"Here I am, Casey. Smell me, taste me, feel me. Anything you like. I'll try not to embarrass you."

She had no idea what he meant by that, but she found his invitation too tempting to refuse. If she went too far for him, he could stop her, couldn't he? She leaned forward. She might never get this chance again.

With the lamp off, the Christmas lights reflected from his eyes and highlighted the planes of his face in a pale, red glow. His lips met hers, slightly open, and she readily parted her own and touched his tongue with hers, an invitation he had no hesitation in answering.

Kalin slanted his head to the side and fitted his body against hers, skillfully manipulating their positions so that they could stretch out together on the sofa. He let go of her wrists and ran both his hands down her sides, examining the way her waist curved in and her hips flared.

"You feel so good." He urged her closer.

Casey deliberately entangled her fingers in the top button of his shirt. He didn't protest, even when she casually moved down his shirt, unbuttoning each button as she went. The thick hair covering his chest called to her, and she speared her fingers through it luxuriously. Her nails raked lightly over his nipples and his breathing quickened, but he didn't stop her.

Emboldened, Casey scooted down to kiss his chest, enjoying the rich aftershave that reminded her of green forests. Kalin's hands locked in her hair, massaging her scalp as he held her against him.

Casey stroked her tongue over each of his flat nipples and felt rewarded when he groaned and rolled to his back so she could torment him with her wildly stroking tongue. Kalin shuddered and groaned and invited her to do it some more.

Since he seemed so responsive to that, she moved up his body to kiss his mouth. At once, his arms went around her like steel bands, locking her there while he kissed her with satisfying desperation. She kissed him several more times, then stroked her hand down his chest for good measure. Kalin groaned her name and begged her not to stop.

The muscles in his arms and chest grew hard and quivered, and when she smoothed her hand across his stomach, the effect was electrifying. His fingers dug into her shoulders. He breathed rapidly, and every other breath was a groan of pleasure with each new way she found to touch him. His pleasure fueled her own, and she found as much enjoyment in her explorations as he did.

She drew back slightly to observe the results of her gentle teasing and saw his eyes slit open to stare back at her. His cheeks flushed, and his eyes glowed in the semi-darkness like dark sapphires.

"Casey?"

She smiled. "You look thoroughly debauched."

"Do I? That's because you're so thorough." He reached up to frame her face with his hands. "Do you think you could kiss me some more?"

She stretched out beside him in answer to his request and kissed him deeply. Kalin shuddered and encouraged her with his response to kiss him again and again. She smoothed her hands over his chest while she kissed him and gloried in the way he groaned and called her name.

When her fingers closed over the zipper of his jeans, his hand covered hers. "Are you sure you want this?"

Casey fought to ignore the chill that settled in her heart. "Granny said I should find out what's holding you back from making love to me now that there's nothing to stop you."

"She did, did she? I'd hate to hear what your grandfather would say to that." He held her close, still breathing hard.

"Well? What is holding you back?"

Kalin laughed breathlessly and buried his nose against her neck. "Precious little. Don't tempt me."

"Why not? I used to love to tempt you. You used to love being tempted." Casey let her fingers wander down his chest once more.

Kalin drew in a shaky breath. "You're just as wanton as you ever were."

The words were spoken in jest, but they fell on Casey's ears with the effect of a chilling arctic blast, withering her desire as if it had never flowered. She curled her fingers into her palm.

Kalin appeared unaware of her withdrawal. "I've been wanting to ask you something." He blew a lock of her hair off her brow. "One of my few cases is coming to trial the day after Christmas, and I'll have to go back to Houston. How about coming over and sitting in the courtroom with me?"

"I don't think so, Kalin."

Something about her voice attracted his attention. "Are you all right?"

"I'm fine, thank you. What's your trial about?"

"Don't do the polite bit on me, when it's obvious I've said or done something. Whatever it was, I didn't mean it the way you're taking it."

Casey studied the way the Christmas lights reflected off the planes of his face. "I don't like being called wanton when all I wanted was to kiss you and touch you."

Kalin lay in silence a moment, absently stroking his hands down her sides. He pulled her closer and cradled her head on his shoulder and combed his fingers through her hair.

He sighed. "If it means anything at all to you, I respond to you exactly the same way you respond to me. All you have to do is touch me, and I'm ready to take you to bed."

"Is that what you were trying to prove? If you want to practice bedroom psychology, pick another victim."

He prevented her movement to roll to a sitting position. "The last thing you are is a victim, Casey Gray. You've allowed a lot of nonsense I said while I was angry to affect your entire outlook. What I want to know is why?"

"Why what?"

"Why has it affected you like this? You would hardly look me in the face at Merrick's party the other night. It was pretty obvious that you'd rather have faced an axe murderer than me."

Casey swallowed hard. His hands held her face tilted so he could look into her eyes.

"Well?" he asked.

"Will you please let me up?"

"It goes back to your mother and how you perceived her behavior. Or how your grandmother perceived her behavior."

She pushed away from him.

"Have you ever talked with your grandmother about it?"

"Granny doesn't even mention my mother's name if she can help it, and I don't care to retard her recovery by forcing her to discuss something she's made it clear is off-limits."

"Casey." He tapped her cheek lightly with his forefinger until she looked up and met his eyes. "You need to talk to someone about it. I'm always here for you."

She forced herself to look at him calmly. "Thank you."

"I wish I could feel you were going to take me up on that."

"Maybe I will."

"I won't hold my breath." He let her go.

Casey sat up and shoved her hair behind her ears.

"I don't like knowing that things I said messed you up like this," Kalin said.

"What makes you think I'm messed up?"

Kalin smiled. "Are you sure you want me to answer that?"

Casey stared at the Christmas tree, almost wishing he hadn't brought it, then at the pile of gifts beneath it.

"I've hurt you enough. The last thing I want is to make you feel I'm trying to compound the injury."

"I believe you." A thought struck her and she began to laugh. She glanced over her shoulder, brimful of laughter, to see Kalin watching her with expectant blue eyes. "Have you ever thought of trying to control me with sex?"

Whatever he'd expected her to say, that wasn't it. His mouth dropped open and his eyes widened. "What?"

"You heard me. A woman who is as wanton as I am would be willing to do almost anything for a tumble in the hay with you."

Kalin stared at her, clearly nonplused. A moment later, he laughed with her. "I don't think I've ever been paid such a high compliment before. I'm glad you think I'm so good in bed."

"Oh, I don't *know* that you're so good in bed," she said in suggestive tones. "But I sure would like to find out."

Kalin smoothed his hand over her shoulder. "There's one thing you're very good at, and that is putting a man on the spot."

"Good. I like the feeling that I'm not the only one always being put on the spot."

"You never were." Kalin pulled her into his arms and hugged her, hard. "Uncle Jack was on my case for weeks about the way I lost my temper in public that time. Even my mother wanted to skin me alive, and usually I'm her blue-eyed boy."

Casey, stunned at this revelation, looked at him.

"Just accept the fact that I suffered over that little incident almost as much as you did," he said roughly, and kissed her.

His kiss was hard and hurting, but healing as well. Casey pressed her body against his and wondered if she could coax him into following her into the bedroom.

Kalin massaged her shoulders. "I'll speak to Uncle Jack about your grandmother. I hear depression is common after a stroke."

Casey accepted the change in subject. "She doesn't seem depressed. She told me exactly what songs she wanted at her funeral. She says there's no sense in pussyfooting around about death, or pretending she's coming home when she isn't."

Kalin rubbed her back. "What did you say?"

"Say? I shut up, of course."

"I'm sorry, Casey. I wish I could do something to help."

Casey smiled. "Believe it or not, you have. Your presence on the scene is tremendously comforting to her."

"Oh? Is that so?"

She leaned back and gave him her sassiest grin. "She thinks you're about to save me from a maiden's worst fate." She chuckled and added, "All this talk about law school has made her nervous."

"What's a maiden's worst fate?" Kalin asked, releasing her.

Casey reminded herself again that Kalin wasn't seriously interested in her. He wanted to assuage his sense of guilt.

She turned away and smiled at him over her shoulder. "Granny thinks the worst thing that can happen to a woman is to die unmarried. Not even the idea that I could become a rich, old maid lawyer is enough to comfort her."

Chapter 9

Kalin walked into Casey's grandmother's hospital room early on the day after Christmas. Alice had finished the egg custard Casey had prepared for her and had dropped off to sleep.

Casey almost dropped the china plate when he appeared in the door. He wore a dark suit and a red tie that accentuated his height and his blue eyes. The sight of him took her breath away.

He scanned her tense face. "Casey, are you all right?" He came closer to look down at her grandmother's sleeping face. "Is she always this still?"

"Yes, that's what worries me. She'll sleep until this afternoon, when her friends arrive to visit."

Kalin folded her in his arms. "Don't worry, sweetheart. Uncle Jack is giving her special attention. Is that a twelve-day weather chart on the wall?" He nodded toward the chart Casey had affixed to the hospital wall the day before in a position where Alice could see it easily.

She nodded. "Granny is thrilled with it. She won't let me forget to make notes of the weather every day."

The chart contained twelve boxes, each with a date and a corresponding month noted on it, and plenty of space for Casey to record each day's weather.

"Lydia is fascinated with the Twelve Days. I'll tell her to drop by. Did you open your present this morning?"

Casey blinked. "I'll open it tonight when I get home."

"Don't forget. I'll call you, okay?"

She nodded.

"Take care of yourself," he said, gave her a quick kiss, and left.

She hastened to the door and watched as he walked down the hall. He had the confident, easy carriage of a natural athlete. The fact that she still loved to watch him disturbed her. She stood in great danger of emotional dependence on Kalin again.

"I keep on telling you," Casey told Bonnie later, as the two sat over lunch at Cap'n Bob's. "We're just good friends."

"Oh, yeah? So where is he?" Bonnie stirred her coffee.

Casey grimaced. "He had to go back to Houston for a trial. He's representing a rape victim in a personal suit against the rapist."

"That's Kalin for you. You ought to go watch him."

"That's what Granny said. She lectured me this morning on making a young man feel admired. It was priceless."

Bonnie waved her coffee cup in a manner that brought one of Casey's newly hired waitresses running with the coffee pot. "Your grandmother is a fountain of wisdom, Casey Gray. You ought to rent a motel room and be in court every day he is. You may never get another chance. I doubt he'll practice much longer."

Casey waited while the waitress refilled Bonnie's cup. "I'd like to, but I have to work and keep an eye on Granny." She lifted her own cup to her lips. "Besides, tomorrow is the tenth anniversary of Derrick Davenport's death, and Kalin will probably think I'm trying to trick him into marrying me or something."

"Casey, that's ridiculous and you know it."

Casey shrugged. "How should I know it? That's what he accused me of before, and all I was guilty of then was not wanting him to leave me."

"He accused you of trying to trick him into marriage?"

Casey shifted and sloshed hot coffee over her fingers. "Yes, he did. He also said I had made him look like a fool."

Bonnie's brown eyes widened. "He said that? Did it occur to you to ask him what he meant?"

"I did, and he said that if I didn't know, it was a waste of time to tell me. What really seemed to get him was all that junk the newspapers printed about my future aspirations." She swallowed coffee and added, "No telling what they'll print this time."

Bonnie looked thoughtfully at her coffee cup, then at Casey. "You mean that stuff about how you were going to study in Paris, and have your own TV cooking show?"

Casey winced.

"Well, you can't blame him. You really did used to lay it on heavy about going off to cooking school and all. Poor old Kalin probably thought you could hardly wait to get away from him and hit the big city." She met Casey's stunned gaze for a moment, then said, "You spent a lot of time convincing Kalin you thought more of earning money to go off to school than you did of him, and now you're surprised because you succeeded."

Casey was simmering gently when Lydia appeared to show her a photocopy of another ad they might run. "Bring her a serving of our new rice dressing," she snapped, thinking the new arrival was their waitress.

"Don't mind her," Bonnie said when Lydia looked startled. "She always gets like this when I point out the flaws in her thinking. You're Kalin's sister, aren't you? I'm Bonnie, Casey's best friend. I used to advise her on how to seduce your brother."

"Please tell her to seduce him thoroughly." Lydia laughed. "He's driving us all crazy."

The moment Lydia returned to the office, Bonnie said, "Now you listen to me, Casey Gray. You're the most loving person I've ever known. But . . . give you a job and you go crazy. Mark my words, Kalin got the impression that you'd rather earn a couple of dollars than be with him."

Casey was insulted. "I like to take time off as well as anyone, but I have certain obligations."

"Right. Cap'n Bob's would collapse. Your grandmother would pick that moment to get worse." Bonnie leaned forward. "Trust me, Casey. No one is indispensable. Forsake this joint and go to Houston. You won't regret it."

*

By the time Casey reached the Houston court where the trial was proceeding and had slipped into a seat at the back of the courtroom, she was already regretting it.

She hadn't changed from her gray wool suit and the pale pink silk blouse she'd worn to work. A sudden warming trend in the weather meant she now felt half-roasted.

Worse, she kept thinking of the duties she left undone or had turned over to the inexperienced Lydia. She took a deep breath and exhaled slowly, then peered around a woman's head for a sight of the protagonists.

Kalin stood before a table with a stack of documents spread out before him and fiercely objected to something the defending attorney said. Even from the back of the courtroom, his blue eyes were easily visible when he turned.

The judge sustained the objection, and Kalin sat down.

Casey watched, fascinated. The Kalin she knew was easygoing and relaxed, rarely raising his voice, and certainly not given to acting.

Kalin, the attorney, reacted with intense emotion to everything the defending attorney said, leaping up to shout objections, and looking about as relaxed as a cat on an electric fence. When he conducted a cross-examination, he did so with vigor, firing questions with a rapidity Casey hadn't guessed he could achieve.

By the time the trial concluded for the day, she professed herself in awe. However much he'd disliked it, Kalin hadn't wasted his time in law school.

She rose with the rest of the spectators and walked slowly forward. Kalin conferred with his client as he packed his papers into his briefcase and didn't see her until she stood about twenty feet from him.

He glanced up and his eyes widened. For a moment he froze, then he hastily excused himself and came toward her.

He gripped her arm, his eyes fairly blazing. "You came. How long have you been here?"

"Yes, and I'm glad I did. I came in at the point where you were objecting to the defense lawyer's attempt to prove your client smoked pot in the tenth grade."

"If we weren't in court, I'd kiss you. You don't have to get back right away, do you?"

"I thought I'd take you to dinner first. I spotted an attractive little Italian restaurant on the way here."

"Great. Wait right here."

Casey watched as he spoke to his client once more, admiring the way his suit outlined his broad shoulders, and how his long, slim hands illustrated something he said.

When he returned, his face was full of anticipation. They walked through the building, which despite its newness, managed to project an air of mahogany walls and ancient stability. Kalin's hand rested at her back in its old, possessive manner, and Casey realized she liked it there.

The restaurant Casey had noticed was hardly more than a hole in the wall of an older building, with warehouses and railroad tracks nearby, but the greenery in the window had caught her eye.

"I enjoyed your performance this afternoon," she told him, sipping wine. "Are you sure you want to quit law?"

"Being a lawyer is almost as bad as being a doctor. Everyone calls you at midnight to get them out of jail." He smiled at her. "If I'd known you were there, I'd have put on the performance of my life."

Casey laughed. "I never knew you could carry on like Perry Mason. It was great."

She let her eyes linger on his face, loving the happiness reflected in the glow of his eyes and the curve of his chiseled mouth. Alice and Bonnie had been right.

"I used to go and watch my father every now and then. He was better than any actor. I just can't do it if I don't believe in my client and my case." He stopped and surveyed her intently, then reached across the table to take her hand. "After dinner, will you come by my apartment? There's something I want to show you."

At the moment, she'd have agreed to almost anything he suggested. She was rewarded by the way he smiled at her.

"By the way," she said slowly, unsure how to phrase her next statement, "I'm going to need a good lawyer. Are you taking new clients, or are you scaling down your practice?"

"Darling, I'll represent you anytime. Whom are we suing?"

"We aren't suing anyone. I spoke to Joe this morning, and I've decided to buy Cap'n Bob's."

Kalin's eyes narrowed and he leaned back in his chair, still holding her hand. "Have you?"

"As you pointed out, Granny will never recover completely. I'll need a job close to home so I can take care of her."

"You mean you can't stand to be left alone with your own thoughts," Kalin regarded her steadily.

Casey flushed with annoyance and tried to pull her hand away. "Forget I mentioned it."

"Don't imagine meanings into things I say." He kept her hand and smiled. "I'm glad to hear you intend to remain in Winnie. I'll handle the sale for you. You're certain this is what you want?"

"I'm certain." Casey straightened as their waiter arrived with their food.

As they ate, Kalin entertained her with a description of some of the cases he'd taken since he began his practice. She listened and laughed, well-pleased that she had listened to Bonnie. Kalin seemed almost like the young man she'd known years ago, loving and eager to share his life with her.

When they left the restaurant, he drove her straight to his apartment in a pink brick building that fronted a busy street. He pulled his SUV into a slot before the end apartment and hustled her up the metal stairs to the end door on the second floor.

Casey stepped inside and glanced around cautiously. The living room was furnished in a casual country style that suited Kalin, and he had every available surface in the room stacked with books and manuscript pages. The sight was so homelike, she smiled and walked forward to sit on the sofa and turn over the top page of the stack of paper reposing on the coffee table.

When she glanced up, her eye fell on a framed map of Galveston Bay with all the best flounder beds marked in red. In the corner of the room, as if he'd dropped them there and had never bothered to move them, he had propped two fly rods and a net. The duck decoy telephone she'd given him for Christmas held a place of honor on an end table.

"Do you like my humble abode, or are you itching to reduce it to a state of unnatural neatness?" He remained standing, watching her examine her surroundings.

"I love it." Casey cast an affectionate glance around the room. "It looks like you."

"I'm glad you think so. Wait until you see my computer setup. You'll be impressed."

"I'm already impressed. You've got all your gear right out here where you can see it." She studied the hunting rifle in its case he had stored behind a padded armchair.

"That's Uncle Jack's. I had it repaired for him at a shop near my office the other day."

She smiled. "Is this another new Western?" She shucked off her wool jacket gratefully.

"Take it home with you and write me one of your famous twenty-page critiques. I'm about ready to send it off, so let's hope it doesn't need a total rewrite." He touched her hair. "Maybe I can sweeten your disposition before you start reading."

Casey glanced at him, wondering at the serious note underlying the teasing words.

He pulled her up to stand beside him. "Come on. I want to

show you something."

She followed willingly and looked with interest around his bedroom. A framed Western landscape hung over the bed, and a pair of flounder gigs were propped against a wall.

Kalin guided her across the room to the corner containing his computer equipment. His printer sat on top of the file cabinet, and his computer occupied a hutch that had a framed photograph sitting on the top shelf.

Casey came closer and saw herself as she had looked during her senior year of high school.

There were several other photographs of her taped on the side of the file cabinet. As she assimilated them, Kalin's arms came around her from behind.

"You may not realize it," he said, "but you're directly responsible for the sale of my first book."

"Me?" She turned her head but couldn't see his face.

He kissed her temple and hugged her. "I kept that picture over my keyboard so I could see it while I worked."

"Next you'll be telling me I inspire you."

"You have no idea. I longed to be able to tell you someday that I sold a book."

Casey heard the smile in his voice. "It was only a matter of time. I always knew you would sooner or later."

"Did you? You had more faith in me than I had in myself. My family never could understand why I wanted to do something as chancy as write Western novels. Neither could I, when I got my first effort back by return mail."

"You reworked it and sent it back out, I hope." Casey leaned her head back to rest it on his shoulder.

"Not right away, I'm afraid. I'd thought it would sell instantly. It was a crushing disappointment when it didn't. Plus, I was in law school at the time and hardly had time to lament, so I set it aside until I graduated."

"I've had recipes like that."

"I know you have, darling." He laughed tenderly and tightened his arms around her. "Remember how hard you used to work on a recipe? You'd test it and retest it, then if it still didn't win the contest or wow the tasters, you'd sit up half the night evaluating it and trying to find out what had gone wrong."

"You thought I was crazy, didn't you?"

"Well, yes," he admitted. "But I figured that if that was what it took, then I'd be crazy, too. What was really behind your success as a cook was a lot of planning and hard work and learning from your mistakes."

"I'll say," Casey agreed.

"I keep your picture by my computer to remind me of that. So you see, you're the real reason I sold my book."

Casey stared at the picture and swallowed. Of all the scenarios she might have predicted, she had never expected Kalin to admit that he thought of her the whole time she was gone.

"Say something, darling." He sounded concerned.

She gulped and blinked rapidly, finding herself quite incapable of admitting she had thought of him equally as often. "I used to dream that after I had become a world-famous chef, I'd perfect a new cheesecake or something you really, really loved, and name it after you."

"Why?" Kalin chuckled and rocked her in his hold.

"For the same reason you kept my picture on your computer, of course. You *inspired* me."

Kalin whipped her around to face him, laughing. "Casey Gray, I'm going to have to punish you for that remark."

"Does this punishment have anything to do with scaling fish or defeathering ducks?"

"No way." He walked her backward toward the bed.

"In that case, do your worst."

Kalin shoved her back and fell beside her on the bed. "You lack a proper attitude of respect for outdoor pursuits."

"You insult my copper bowls all the time."

He leaned over her. "That is not on a par with baiting a fish hook with a leaf when the fish are lining up to bite."

Casey propped her arms between them and pretended to try to hold him off. "You're right. Insulting a cook's copper bowl deserves the death penalty. How would you like to die?"

"In your arms." Kalin kissed her.

Casey took fire instantly. She wrapped her arms around his neck and moaned deep in her throat as Kalin kissed her and crushed her down into the mattress.

The swiftness of her own response startled her. She had let herself fall back into loving Kalin and had forgotten the need to maintain control over her traitorous body at all times.

She tried, but it was no use. She couldn't think while she was in Kalin's arms—her body ruled her mind.

Kalin had responded to her soft moan with shuddering pleasure, and now he kissed her again while lying fully on top of her and pressing her into the mattress with his weight. She dug her nails into his shoulders and arched her back, gasping. Every vestige of her control fell away.

He stroked his hands down the front of her pink silk blouse, undoing buttons. The moment he touched her bare skin, Casey arched toward him, using her body to beg for his possession in all the ways she'd once enticed him. Kalin removed her bra and blouse. She cried out and twisted wildly beneath him, while he used his mouth to tantalize her with a foreshadowing of what was to come.

She acquired a grip on his hair that he didn't loosen as he worked off her skirt and slip. Kalin managed to sit up and admire the slim body he had undressed without dislodging her fingers. He stripped off his own clothing swiftly and lay beside her, still entwined in her arms and wearing nothing but the tan that stopped at his waistline.

Casey, enthralled with the sensations flooding every nerve ending, ran her fingers down his back and encountered no clothing. The discovery electrified her. She explored him with her hands in all the ways he explored her.

"Casey," he whispered. "You make me go crazy."

His voice shook as much as he did. The sound of it made her want to cry with ecstasy.

"Please, please do," she said, and groaned.

Now was the time for him to draw back if he intended to. In some dim corner of her mind, she waited for him to push away from her, but this time he didn't.

This time, he took her all the way, and Casey almost cried with the ecstasy they created together. For all the dreaming she had done about making love to Kalin, none of her daydreams came anywhere close to the real thing. She knew now she had never felt anything as powerful as the intimacy of being with him like this or the knowledge of being one with the man she loved.

Surely, she thought, in the warm aftermath, with his arms around her and her head lying on his shoulder, Kalin still loved her.

She still loved him. She admitted it to herself, lying beside him in the deepening twilight. She wondered if anything would ever come of it.

Not likely, she decided, struggling to be realistic. Probably, he just wanted to prove to her, and to himself, that she was not irreparably damaged by the events of five years ago.

If she had any sense at all, she told herself, she would make it as easy as possible for Kalin to fade out of her life now that he had proved his point.

*

Casey spent the next morning in the kitchen under Lydia's worshipful eye, concocting a dessert she claimed would win worldwide fame for Cap'n Bob's.

"It's a recipe I've saved for years." She crumbled chocolate cookies with a rolling pin. "That man from Beaumont, the one who beat me in the Rice Contest, invented it. He called it 'Deep Dark Secret,' and I think I'll keep the name."

Lydia stared at the yellowed newspaper clipping Casey consulted. "So that's him. Wow. This recipe is really rich."

"People love cheesecake—the richer, the better. Just wait until tonight. I'll have to cut slices so thin . . . "

Lydia grinned. "Too bad Kalin's not here. He loves cheesecake." She looked up, suddenly serious. "I've never said this to anyone, Casey, but I was glad when my father died. Then I felt guilty for feeling relieved and went to pieces, in Kalin's arms, unfortunately. He . . . he was very . . . upset."

Lydia's hesitant words, and her woebegone expression suddenly struck a chord in Casey. She stopped crushing cookies. "Have you been feeling all this time that it was your fault Kalin broke up with me?"

Lydia's soft eyes filled with tears despite her brave attempt to cover them. "Well, wasn't it? I think he could have faced all the bad things my father had done in business, but when I told him all the things Dad had been saying to me and to Mom, he . . . he . . . " She stopped and turned away.

Casey reached out at once. "Lydia, it wasn't your fault Kalin got mad at me. There were a lot of things wrong between us." She drew the younger woman close and hugged her.

"Things like who your father really was?" Lydia buried her face against Casey's neck and hugged her back. "I wish Derrick Davenport had been my father. It's better never to have known him than to have to remember him saying terrible things. I almost hated him by the time he died."

It seemed Kalin had told his family all about her, so much so that they considered her one of the family.

"I doubt your father knew what he was saying. He must have been sick for some time before he died. And don't blame yourself anymore. Our breakup wasn't your fault at all."

It was her own, Casey realized, as she taught Lydia the art of creaming sugar and butter and cream cheese. She had been determined to prove she wasn't like her mother, and rather than tell Kalin why she felt so driven, she'd concealed her history from him until the tabloids exposed it at the worst possible time.

She poured the cheese batter into the large, three-inch tall casing she'd prepared. Kalin had understood her motives better than she had. She dealt with other responsibilities and thought about it all morning. The impression she received of herself was not a pretty one.

"Your office phone has been ringing off the hook," Lydia said later. "So I answered it. It's Kalin, and he's fussing a blue streak, but I can't understand a thing he's saying. Something about did you open a Christmas present last night."

Casey smiled and wiped cookie crumbs off her hands. "I didn't have time." Because she had driven in from Houston early that morning and stopped only long enough to change clothes.

Memories of the night before brought a smile to her lips as she hurried to her little office and grabbed the receiver. She nearly dropped it when Kalin's angry voice spoke in her ear.

"It's about time you answered the phone, Casey Gray. Where the hell have you been? Hiding out?"

He sounded furious. Casey felt as if her heart froze into lifelessness. "I was in the kitchen making a cheesecake. Why?"

"I gather you haven't read the latest issue of *Star Shines*," he said in tones Casey last heard five years ago.

Star Shines was a garish tabloid dedicated to the lives and scandals of celebrities, especially Hollywood stars.

Casey noted the contempt and fury that mingled in his voice. "I never read it," she said. "Why . . . ? Oh."

The Davenport death anniversary. She had forgotten it.

"That's right," Kalin said. "Oh."

"What did they say?" She ignored hollow emptiness in her

stomach. Or was it her heart that had suddenly gone empty?

"What didn't they say is more like it. I should have thought once was enough for you. What I want to know is why did you have to drag me into it?"

At that moment, Bonnie appeared in the office door with a copy of *Star Shines* in her hand, open to a page headlined, "Davenport Love-Child Retains Lawyer: Plans to Sue Davenport Estate."

Casey grabbed for the paper. "Just a minute, Kalin."

"Is this your way of increasing the business at Cap'n Bob's?" Kalin snapped.

Casey scanned the headline and photos. Hers hailed from her high school annual, and Kalin's seemed to be of the same order.

"What do you mean?" She couldn't seem to think.

"If you think you're going to involve me in any of your future plans, you're crazy."

He drew in a breath to say more, but Casey's brain finally caught up with her ears.

"Go to hell, Kalin McBryde." She slammed down the phone.

"Oh, wow," Bonnie murmured, exchanging glances with Lydia.

Casey scowled. "Just look at this nonsense."

"Casey," Bonnie said, in an insistent voice.

The telephone rang once more.

Casey picked it up, her attention still focused on the story. "Cap'n Bob's. *Drop dead, Kalin.*" She slammed the phone down.

She realized suddenly that Bonnie had collapsed into the one chair the office boasted, covering her face with her hands and moaning with laughter. Glancing up, Casey froze. Elizabeth McBryde and Annie Johnson stood just outside the door. Both looked enthralled.

Casey set her chin and glared once more at the story.

The premise was simple, although it required several columns of lurid type to spell it out. Casey, who now called herself Casey Davenport, had retained the son of famous criminal attorney Walter McBryde to sue the Davenport estate. She intended to dispossess

Davenport's widow of every penny and get herself recognized as Davenport's daughter and legal heir. If McBryde failed to win her inheritance, she intended to become a lawyer herself and spend the rest of her life attempting to right a great wrong.

"Oh, no." Casey gasped, forgetting her audience. "It says I intend to avenge my teenage mother for the way Davenport treated her by disinheriting his legal wife."

The telephone rang once more. Casey reached behind it to unplug the plastic connector. The phone fell silent.

"You may as well talk to him," Elizabeth McBryde said. "Kalin will call every telephone in your vicinity until you do."

"I'm never speaking to him again." Casey frowned fiercely.

"Oh, yeah?" Bonnie grinned and winked at Lydia.

"I mean it," Casey said through clenched teeth. "How dare he suggest I told a reporter all this—this nonsense?"

"Did he say that?" Bonnie rolled her eyes. "Poor old Kalin must be in total shock."

Casey remembered Kalin's mother and flushed. "Well, so am I. I'm sorry about this, but I had nothing to do with it."

She had no real hope of being believed, but Elizabeth stunned her by saying, "He knows that. Or he will when he calms down and starts thinking. Kalin has always hated this kind of thing."

Casey recalled that Elizabeth McBryde's father had been Conrad Kalin, a maverick congressman from West Texas whose claim to fame was his resistance to the McCarthy era probes.

The unexpected kindness undermined the remains of her bravado. Tears fell on the paper in her hands.

Lydia offered Casey a tissue. "The dining room phone is ringing now. How much do you want to bet it's Kalin?"

One of her new waiters appeared in the doorway. "There's a man on the phone out front. He says you'd better come talk to him or else."

Casey reared up her head. "Tell him he's fired. I've decided to become a lawyer myself so I can sue both him *and* the Davenport estate."

Chapter 10

Casey left her cheesecake unfinished and her duties at the restaurant unattended. She wanted to inform her grandmother of the article before her afternoon visitors arrived.

As for Kalin McBryde, she swore she was never speaking to him again as long as she lived.

So much for sex, she thought, blinking away more tears. Wonderful as it was, it sure hadn't solved the problems that kept Kalin from loving her again. She needed to forget him and get back to her original dream.

Whatever it had been, she thought, passing the spreading rice fields she had loved since childhood. All her dreams now seemed to include Kalin, and she had no idea how that had happened.

Alice insisted upon having the entire piece read to her. Casey did so, careful to keep any emotion out of her voice.

When she had finished, Alice studied Casey thoughtfully. "Have you informed that young man about it?"

"Actually, he informed me."

"Is that so?" Alice smiled grimly. "Took in bad part, did he? Well, you can't blame him. Figuring in the tabloid press isn't what the McBrydes are used to."

Casey forbore mentioning the constant harassment of Conrad Kalin and his family during the McCarthy hearings. "No, Granny."

"You didn't talk to these people, I hope."

"No, Granny."

Alice sighed. "Well, Casey, I'm sorry for you. It looks as though you'll suffer for your mother's sins after all, in spite of all I did to keep you out of it." She turned her head to look at her granddaughter. "I've never had to be ashamed of you. Ewing and I have always been proud of you."

"Have you, Granny? I'm glad." Casey's voice was husky with feeling. "I used to long to hear you say that."

"And now that you're hearing it, you'd rather not?" Alice regarded her with grim humor. "My time here is short. Every night I dream of Ewing. Yes, and of Cynthia. It's time you knew that you made up to us for any suffering Cynthia caused us. We were both terrified when I walked in the house with you in my arms twenty-three years ago. We'd just buried our only child, who'd brought us nothing but grief, and there we were, beginning all over again with Cynthia's baby."

Casey had never thought of her childhood from this angle. No wonder Alice and Ewing had been so strict with her, and so determined to teach her values and good work habits.

"You were a good child. Not like Cynthia." Alice's eyelids began to droop. "Maybe we were too lax with her."

"I can't imagine you being lax, Granny."

"I don't suppose you can," Alice said. "We didn't think we could afford to be with you."

Casey swiped away tears and said nothing.

"I always hoped you'd marry that young man and live here," Alice went on. "He loved the country, and once, he loved you."

"I know, Granny," Casey said.

"You killed his love for you." Her eyes closed. "I tried to warn you. Work has its place, but a man expects to come first."

Casey winced at the thought that she had killed Kalin's love for her. "If I didn't work, I would turn out like my mother, so I worked too much."

Alice went on as if she hadn't heard. "A young man needs to know he's Number One. It's part of his makeup as a man. You never gave him that."

Casey said nothing, but memories of arguing with Kalin over taking a day off from her job arose in her mind.

"I saw it coming," Alice said. "It was an explosive situation for a young man in love, and you were too busy with your own plans to give him what he needed. I was sorry to see it, but you deserved what happened, Casey." Alice's eyes closed, and she appeared to be drifting off to sleep. "You kept on talking about cooking school. As if *that* would keep you warm on a cold night."

Stunned, Casey stared at the opposite wall.

Alice's head dropped to the side, and her breathing became deep and regular.

Casey drew in a quivering breath and dabbed at her eyes with the tissue Lydia had given her. It seemed she had failed Kalin in many ways, and her grandmother had stored them up to tell her about them when it was far too late to do anything about it.

Casey did what she always did in times of trouble. She set her chin and went back to Cap'n Bob's, where she dealt with every problem facing her in double-quick time and perfected a cheesecake that would electrify the entire state of Texas.

"Merrick just called," Lydia said. "She says not to forget that you're taking the LSAT test tomorrow in Houston."

"Houston," Casey snarled.

Lydia scrambled behind the chopping island in the center of the kitchen, laughing. "She's bringing over a map of the location, and you're supposed to get a really good night's sleep."

Casey clapped a hand to her forehead. "I don't have time for this. Why did I ever start this law school business?"

"So you can outscore Kalin?"

"Ah. I knew there was a good reason." Casey stripped off her apron and tossed it aside. "It's all yours. You've just been promoted, by the way. You are now assistant chef and manager."

Lydia looked thrilled. "Wait until I tell Mom."

Casey went home and stalked into the living room to plug in her Christmas tree as she did every night. To her shock, one of the still-wrapped presents suddenly emitted a loud ring tone. She found it and tore off the wrapping.

"A smart phone," she breathed, staring at the small, lit-up object in dismay.

It looked like an expensive, up-to-date model, with applications already loaded and very likely, numbers already programmed into it. It ceased ringing abruptly, and Casey found the button that would turn it off.

She was not ready for another cell phone yet, she thought, shuddering. She supposed she'd have to get one sooner or later, but she preferred to make it later. Much later, when Kalin no longer cared to call her on it.

But she slipped the little phone into her purse the next morning, still turned off, and drove to Houston after her morning visit to the hospital and her stop by Cap'n Bob's to give Lydia the day's list of tasks.

She arrived at the testing site and took a seat before a computer. To her surprise, Casey enjoyed the test, even though it covered many things she knew nothing about. But reasoning from a few given facts was something a cook excelled at. Perhaps she'd win a scholarship to law school. That would frost old Kalin McBryde.

The thought of frosting Kalin bucked her up, even though the test took the better part of the day. By the time Casey exited the building and found the parking lot, her head pounded with exertion and the winter afternoon sun sat low in the sky.

"Well? How was it?"

Casey glanced up, startled. Kalin's SUV was parked beside her rental car, and he leaned on her fender smiling at her, still dressed in the suit he'd worn in court.

She frowned and tried to remember why she was mad at him. "How on earth did you find me?"

"It wasn't hard." He pushed off the fender and came toward her, scanning her tired face. "You look like hell."

"Thanks. That was some test, plus I didn't sleep well."

"If you want to blame it on me, I'll have to shut up. I started to come apologize in person last night, but Merrick begged me not to disturb you before the test."

"It doesn't matter." She turned toward her car.

He took her arm and turned her to face him. "It does matter. If I caused you to lose more sleep—don't cry, darling."

"I'm not crying." Her words were muffled against his suit jacket. "I'm tired, and my head hurts, and I'm starving."

"I know, darling. Leave your car here. There's a restaurant you'll love nearby."

He helped her into his SUV, then climbed in beside her and held her a moment. "I'm sorry I accused you of talking to *Star Shines*. I should have known better."

"It doesn't matter," Casey repeated. "This will probably happen every time there's a Derrick Davenport anniversary. Now they seem to have decided I really am his daughter."

Kalin sighed. "I don't suppose it would help if I explained that I had to take an awful ribbing from every lawyer and judge at the courthouse yesterday morning. What really got me was that I had no idea that article was on the newsstand."

"Neither had I," Casey said.

"I know. I'm sorry, darling. Sit back and rest. You need food before I can expect to get any sense out of you."

She leaned back. "That test was horrendous. Everyone looked so rested and *smart*. Merrick will never live it down if I flunk."

Kalin chuckled. "With your analytical abilities? I expect you to be in the top ten percent." He kissed her lightly. "Look, Casey, I'm sorry I yelled at you yesterday. You might at least have given me a chance to apologize."

She smiled wearily. "I was in no mood to listen to apologies. Nothing would have been abject enough."

He laughed and studied her face in the pale, late afternoon sunlight. "It's happening all over again, isn't it?"

She stared back at him. "What is?"

"One of these days, you're going to need a keeper."

"For what?"

"To make sure you go to bed and stay there, for one thing." He started the car, then buckled on his seat belt thoughtfully.

"Are you applying for the position?"

"Not likely," he said, and set the vehicle in motion.

Casey went cold all over and said nothing. It was a good thing she was too tired to care that Kalin no longer loved her.

Kalin parked on a quiet street and ushered her inside a small Italian restaurant, where he seated her quickly and ordered appetizers and wine.

Casey sipped the wine and studied him while he checked an incoming call on his phone. His long lashes veiled his eyes as he frowned over the message then returned the phone to his pocket.

Maybe she'd be better off getting another lawyer. "Do you want to forget handling the purchase of Cap'n Bob's for me?" she asked.

The bright azure eyes focused on her immediately. "I've already been in touch with Joe." He tasted his own wine. "I should have the papers ready for your signature early next week."

Just like that. "Thanks a lot for keeping me updated."

"I get tired of hearing about nothing but your damned restaurant." He shrugged. "I liked it better when you were spending every waking moment plotting to beat that man from Beaumont in all the cooking contests."

"My conversation must have been *very* boring to a man who preferred to discuss the various and sundry ways a fish can find to hide itself on the bottom of a lake."

Kalin laughed and reached for her hand. "I wasn't that boring. Sometimes I even discussed the ways a duck can find to land at every lake in a hundred mile radius but the one where my blind was located."

"Sometimes I talked about the weather," Casey said.

"Speaking of the weather, how's your chart coming along?"

"So far, January, February, and March look like good months."

"Have you been opening your presents?"

"Of course I have. Thanks for the phone." She fished it from her purse and held it out to him.

He took it, examined it a moment, frowning, and pressed a button. "No wonder. Why didn't you turn it on?"

She gave him her most innocent stare. "I couldn't find the right button."

"With the box and instructions included? Your nose will grow if you keep on telling lies, Casey Gray." He said nothing else about the phone, other than to adjure her to give the number to the hospital in case her grandmother's condition changed.

"By the way, thanks for the tackle box and all the pretty little feathery things to go in it." She stowed the phone back in her purse.

"Those are called flies."

"No kidding. I thought they were baby birds."

"You're going to learn how to cast a fly if it's the last thing I ever teach you."

They spent the remainder of the evening arguing over the merits of fishing, and Casey enjoyed herself tremendously. She hadn't argued with anyone over fishing in years. Five years, to be exact. It was amazing how she'd missed it.

She didn't feel bereft until Kalin drove her back to her car. The lingering kisses he gave her did nothing to assuage the feeling. Even though he followed her until he saw her get on the freeway safely, she felt almost as if he had deserted her.

*

Casey didn't have long to feel bereft. New Year's Eve approached, and the problems facing her escalated. She could hardly talk to Kalin on the cell phone he had given her without constantly being interrupted by employees. Reporters called for several days in search of exclusive interviews with the alleged Davenport love-child.

The more Casey denied Derrick Davenport, the more determined the reporters were to believe he was her father.

She stalked back out to the big dining area, where all the tables had been crowded toward the walls to leave the central area bare, creating a makeshift dance floor. Supervising the hanging of giant, paper crawfish and alligators was a lot better than speculating on what Kalin was doing in Houston, and whether or not he had truly given up on loving her.

On New Year's Eve, every available table and the small dance floor teemed with customers, and Casey, wearing a red bandanna-print dress, waited tables alongside Lydia and the entire wait staff.

Kalin walked in about nine in the evening, and Casey spotted his tall, jean-clad form at once. Her heart pumped harder at the sight of his tanned face and the steady blue eyes that searched the crowd. Before she could move toward him, a blond cowgirl attached herself to his arm.

To Casey's outrage, he followed the blond toward the dance floor.

She could care less who he danced with, she told herself, and promptly began setting soft drinks at a table of rowdy cowboys who had ordered beer. By the time she had straightened out that mess, Kalin had vanished.

"What the hell do you think you're doing?"

His voice came from behind her, and Casey almost dropped the heavy tray loaded with beer. She wished he didn't remind her so much of one of his own Western heroes.

"Helping out." She forced a smile. "On a night like this, it's all hands on deck."

Kalin regarded her, frowning. "You look tired."

Not a word about the red dress she'd worn with him in mind. "Thanks. With all the confusion tonight, it's hard to remember who ordered what."

The band played a Cajun waltz, which added to the noise. And if she planned to fill the place this full in the future, she'd have to see about some fans to assist with the ventilation.

"You need to step outside a minute." Kalin lifted the tray from her shoulder. "Where does this go?"

"That corner table," she said, before recalling that particular table belonged to Kalin's cousin Merrick and her boyfriend, Clayton Rowe.

She lacked the energy to worry about it, she realized, suddenly stricken by a wave of nausea. She shoved her way through the crowd and practically ran outside, where she leaned against a car until the dizziness passed off.

"Better?" Kalin's voice was quiet and soothing.

He took her arm and led her down a row of pickup trucks and cars to his SUV. Unlocking the door, he helped her in and came around to sit beside her. Casey, grateful for the blessed quiet and fresh air, leaned her head back and closed her eyes.

Kalin sat beside her in silence a moment. "Why do you keep doing this to yourself? Don't you know it upsets me to see you looking so stressed and worn?"

Her eyes popped open. "There must be a dozen blond cowgirls inside who'd love to soothe your feelings."

Kalin smiled. She could see the expression, thanks to her foresight in having the burned-out parking lot lights replaced.

"Is that so? I'm surprised I'm not getting a lecture from you about spending New Year's Eve in the law library or at the computer."

Casey blinked, confused. "Oh. Well. Let me think on it a bit and get wound up properly. Although, now that you mention it, a few weekends at your computer would do more to help the duck population than all the money you probably contribute to Ducks Unlimited."

Kalin chuckled and drew her close. "Forget I mentioned the matter."

Casey sighed as Kalin's lips touched hers and his hands stroked her unresisting body. She slid her arms around his neck, holding him to her and letting him take his fill of her kisses. Memories of their night together made her tremble.

A fine tremor in Kalin's hands attracted her attention, and his breathing quickened. She sought to increase both by kissing his ear and nibbling his earlobe.

Kalin drew back suddenly. "We'd better go back in. I'd keep you out here all night if I could."

"I'm in the mood to let you."

"It's a bit late for that, don't you think?"

Casey felt as if he had stabbed her. She leaped from the vehicle and hurried back down the row of cars.

Kalin caught up to her. "What's your hurry?"

Casey sucked in her breath. "I've got things to see to, and Lydia is alone with everything. Goodbye, Kalin."

"I'm not leaving yet."

Casey glanced fleetingly at him as they passed beneath one of the big arc lights. "I'll tell Lydia to find you a chair at Merrick's table."

Kalin caught her arm, whirled her to face him, and smiled the kind of smile Casey imagined one of his Western heroes would direct at a cattle rustler. "I'm here to see you, and well you know it."

Casey refused to flinch. "Maybe you'd better leave while you still can. I warned you that I was on the lookout for a potentially famous author or a future rich criminal lawyer."

Kalin laughed and threw an arm across her shoulders to hug her lightly. "Since I'm not likely to be either, I suppose that lets me out."

"You should know."

"By the way, I won my case."

Casey stared at the ground as Kalin opened the door for her. "Congratulations, Kalin." She forced a smile. "You may become a rich attorney yet. I'd better keep you on my list just in case."

"Do that." He ushered her back inside the restaurant.

Someone called Kalin's name and he turned aside to greet a friend. The moment he turned, Casey felt an arm slide around her waist from behind.

Clayton Rowe, slightly the worse for the beer he'd ingested, grinned down at her. "Hi, babe. How about a New Year's kiss?" He pulled her toward him.

She planted her hands on his chest and stiff-armed him, but he used one hand to bend her arms at the elbow and reeled her in, still smiling. Crushed in his arms, Casey turned her face aside and ducked her head. In a few minutes, he'd give up on her and go after fresh prey.

"Let go of her, Rowe," Kalin said coldly.

"Get lost, McBryde."

The next instant, Casey felt Clay peeled from her like a recalcitrant bit of plastic wrap. She staggered and almost fell as Clay's chin came into contact with Kalin's right fist. Clay stumbled back into the wall and slumped down it, landing in a relaxed, sitting position with his eyes closed.

Kalin grabbed Casey's wrist and hauled her through the crowd and out the front entrance after one disgusted glance at Clay.

She planted her heels. "Let me go, Kalin McBryde. I've had enough macho behavior for one night."

"You need a keeper. I'm about ready to elect myself, whether you like it or not."

He pulled her out the side door, not slowed at all by her resistance, and stopped in the shadows of the building.

Casey blinked, not quite following this speech. "I don't need a keeper to deal with men who have had too much to drink. In another few seconds, he'd have let go of me on his own."

"Well, he didn't do it fast enough for me, and you look too damned tired to fight back."

She tried to free her wrist. "You're hurting me."

He closed the small distance between their bodies, crushing her breasts against his chest as he locked her against him. His lips came down on hers in a ruthless, plundering, marauding action Casey had never associated with Kalin before. When the kiss ended, she was breathless and trembling.

Kalin trembled also. She could feel his tension as his eyes searched hers.

"Well?" he said. "Don't you want to fight me? Or are you too worn out?"

She had no idea what he was talking about. "Why should I want to fight you? Although you were a little rough."

His hands closed on her shoulders. "There's more to come."

Casey tried to pull back, but he held her in place by merely tightening his grip.

"See what I mean? You're stressed out and dead tired. How do you think it makes me feel to see you like this? If I had my way, you'd be locked in your bedroom for a week."

"With you?" She tried to smile.

"No way. Do you think I want to contribute to your breakdown? The trouble with you is you're still trying to prove to everyone that you're not like your mother. Hold still. I told you there was more to come."

Casey tried in vain to wrench herself from his hold. "I don't have to listen to you."

"As soon as you can get up the energy to break my hold, you're free." His blue eyes were dark with mockery in the fluorescent glow cast by the overhead lighting. "In the meantime, you can listen to my list of complaints, which has changed remarkably little in the past five years."

"Let me go, damn you," Casey fought his grip in vain.

"You're still trying to live down what you see as your mother's sins. I didn't understand that five years ago. That's why the things I said hurt you so badly that you couldn't even write me a simple letter for five years or look me in the face."

"Let go of me."

"And you still think that if you don't work double-time, everyone will think you're a lazy tramp looking for a rich man to take care of you, just like your mother."

Casey swung at him with her open palm, but Kalin blocked her easily by tilting up an elbow.

"It never has occurred to you that maybe what happened to your mother was more Derrick Davenport's fault than it was hers. In fact, I'd call a man who publicly repudiated his daughter a downright bastard. The only sensible thing you've ever done was refuse to acknowledge him as your father."

Casey shoved at his chest with all her might. For all the good it did, she could just as well have shoved at the wall of Cap'n Bob's.

"As for your moral judgment calls on your mother, where do you get off thinking she was lazy? Most kids hate chores. As for tramp, how do you know she slept with any man other than Derrick Davenport, whom she loved?"

"Stop it, damn you." Casey struggled wildly and swung at him once more. "Leave me alone."

"I've designated myself your official keeper, whether you like it or not. My next step is going to be attention to your health, which appears to be in jeopardy at the moment."

"My health is perfect. Let go of me."

"Sorry. That command does not compute. Now let's get into the subject of your physical response to me. How many other men do you go crazy for in bed?"

"Let me go. I hate men."

Kalin held her still. When she tried to kick him, he jerked her into his arms and held her despite her attempts to escape.

"Your desperation belies you, my love. Cut that out, Casey Gray, or I'll have to prove you're a liar. Do you know how I'll do that? I'm so glad you asked. I'll begin by kissing you. After you start getting interested in that, I'll unbutton your dress." He brought one hand around to tease the top button of her red dress. "Then I'll touch you, and you'll make that funny sound you always make, and the next thing I know, you'll be all over me."

Casey panted and fought. "You're mighty sure of yourself,

Kalin McBryde." Just hearing what he'd do made her feel weak.

Kalin laughed and lifted her off her feet. "With you, I am. The bad thing is you don't seem to understand that my physical response to you is precisely the same. For instance, if you really wanted to shut me up, you'd start by kissing me. After I got interested in that, you could unbutton my shirt and touch me. Once you had me in a thoroughly weakened condition from that—"

"I'll weaken you." She tried to hook his leg with her foot.

"No, darling. You're going about it all wrong." He laughed in earnest now, and it infuriated Casey. "You're supposed to kiss me instead of kick me. Maybe I haven't made myself totally clear."

She pinched his arm.

"You want proof? Coming right up." He tightened his grip.

Casey could hardly breathe. She saw his intent too late to turn her face aside. The next instant his lips covered hers. He kissed her until she forgot she wanted to kill him. A few seconds later she forgot her anger and progressed to the stage of wishing he'd touch her all over. She clung desperately to him.

Kalin lifted his head and stared at her. "You see? This is why I can't walk away from you, even though I know I'm courting disaster, that you'll always find a reason to run off to work, or you'll think the restaurant is more important than our problems. Believe me, I wish I could walk away."

He let go of her and stepped back.

Stunned, Casey leaned against the wall and stared at him.

"I'm going," Kalin said. "Otherwise, I'll stay and say a few more things I'm sure you're dying to hear." He backed slowly away. "Oh, and by the way," he added. "Tomorrow's a holiday. Do you know what that is? Be ready tomorrow morning. You're due a lesson in fly casting." He turned and walked away, down the rows of cars.

Too late, Casey found her voice. She yelled after his departing vehicle, "I'm not going fishing with you. I'm too busy studying for law school."

Chapter 11

Casey finished out the night in a daze of exhaustion—both emotional and physical—and fell into bed at dawn. After sleeping a few hours, she arose, cooked a tempting cheese casserole for her grandmother's breakfast, and drove to the hospital.

"How are you and that young man coming along?" Alice asked as Casey unpacked the breakfast box and arranged the items on one of Alice's Blue Willow plates.

Dr. Johnson had just entered the room, so Casey tried evasive tactics. "We're just friends, Granny."

She carried the plate to the over-bed table and arranged it artistically before rolling it into position.

"Hummph," Alice grumbled. "And if that's more custard, I'm not eating it. Cook me some of those pecan pancakes your young man used to like. If an old woman can't eat what she wants during her last days, the world's in a pretty mess."

Casey glanced up, caught the doctor's sympathetic smile, and maintained a straight face. "Tomorrow morning, Granny."

"Well? Are you going to marry him or not? Half the town is laying bets on whether he can attract your attention away from that silly restaurant long enough to consider his proposal."

Casey almost choked. "Granny, Kalin hasn't asked me to marry him, and I doubt if he will."

"I want you to live in my house," Alice said, as if Casey hadn't spoken. "Jack Johnson says Kalin loves this area, and I don't like what city life has done to you."

Casey groaned mentally and spooned up a bite of the cheese casserole for Alice, thankful she hadn't cooked a custard.

"And don't let him give you one of those frippery diamond

engagement rings. The stone will wind up in someone's breakfast biscuit one morning, and then where will you be?"

"You're right, Granny."

"If you get married in the next few days, I can tell Jack to set me up with a wheelchair so I can be at the church."

"Granny, I am not getting married. Besides, Kalin is pleading a case in court, so he can't oblige you, either."

"I've already told you how I feel about couples living together."

"Don't worry." Casey laid out a napkin.

"You'd better worry that I don't recover the use of my good right hand, young lady."

Casey grinned and backed off. "If that's what it takes to get you well, I hope you do."

Alice subsided, although she maintained her stern expression. "Love has to be whole-hearted if it's going to survive the hard times."

"Yes, Granny."

Alice's skin suddenly took on a gray tinge that frightened Casey into motioning the doctor toward the bedside.

"If you can't forgive him, you're better off unmarried the rest of your days." The old woman's words slurred.

"Don't talk anymore, Granny. Just rest."

Alice began to cough, struggling to say something else. Dr. Johnson shooed Casey aside and pushed the call button. Casey, standing in the farthest corner of the room out of the way, felt fear clutch her heart as Alice faded into unconsciousness.

Casey later recalled the week following as a series of vignettes: Kalin standing beside Alice's bed in his favorite jeans and plaid flannel shirt; Kalin appearing every night with coffee in paper cups and food he'd picked up on the way over from Houston; Kalin, still wearing the suit he'd worn in court, holding her in his lap while she dozed with her head on his shoulder.

Dr. Johnson didn't mince words when he told Casey that Alice had suffered another stroke, and that the old woman was now in a coma she would probably never emerge from.

Casey closed her eyes and felt Kalin's arms go around her. He asked the questions she needed answered when she was too stricken to ask them herself and supported her as she heard the answers.

"I'll bring you a comfortable chair," Kalin said gently, as Casey stood, trembling, in his arms. "You'll probably want to be here most of the time. You might as well be comfortable."

She nodded, unable to speak.

Kalin's hand smoothed her hair. "Did you open your Christmas present this morning?"

Drawing in a shaky breath, Casey forced herself to speak through the closure of her throat. "I always open it at night. Thanks for the chair, by the way."

Last night's gift had been an aluminum lawn chair, suitable for pier or bank fishing.

"That's for the fishing trip you're going to invite me on," he said.

Casey smiled, suddenly feeling better. "I'll bet I can guess what tonight's long - skinny - package - that's - shaped - like - a - fishing - rod contains."

"I've always said you were sharp." He kissed her brow lightly. "I'll bet you aced the LSAT."

"Don't remind me of that stupid test. I must have been crazy to let Merrick railroad me into actually taking it."

His blue eyes were tender in his lean, tanned face, and his thick brows made straight, relaxed slashes across his forehead.

She added, "I was having delusions of adequacy."

"What?"

"It gave me great pleasure to daydream about outscoring you."

"Keep on dreaming, sweetheart. You can outscore me anytime," Kalin said, chuckling. "When you get your law degree, you can come into my office. I need a partner like you."

She returned to Alice's bedside, realizing that with Kalin sitting beside her, holding her hand and watching over her with concern, she would never feel alone.

However, she felt like a zombie the rest of the time. She turned daily operations at Cap'n Bob's over to Lydia, who showed surprising talent for restaurant management so long as Casey gave her detailed instructions every morning. Even with the restaurant off her mind, she found she still couldn't rest well.

All Alice's friends, and many of Casey's, shared Casey's bedside vigil. Flowers and cards filled the small room, many mentioning things Casey had baked the senders years before.

Kalin appeared every evening to bully her into leaving Alice's bedside long enough to eat. Then he would sit beside her far into the night, entertaining her with tales of his practice, or just being with her.

She read his new manuscript and wrote him a short critique on it. Reading his latest novel made her feel almost as though she had something to do with his success, and most of the two pages she wrote praised his writing and the story.

"I never thought I'd get encouragement of this sort from you," he said. "Are you sure it was my manuscript you read?"

The following evening, he brought her a rough draft of his latest effort and laid it on Alice's bedside table.

"Tell me about your fishing trips with your grandparents," he said. "Your grandfather told me himself that he taught you how to bait a hook and watch a cork."

Casey pretended ignorance. "Grandpa was a busy man. He didn't have time to fish."

"The guy who won the bass tournament at Lake Sam Rayburn didn't have time to fish?"

Thus encouraged, Casey recounted the tale of her grandfather's win. She loved talking about her memories with someone who comprehended that she was about to lose the bulwark of her childhood. But she could tell him almost nothing about her mother, or her mother's childhood.

Kalin sighed and kissed her forehead. "That's too bad, darling.

Talking to people who knew her as a child would probably give you a whole new outlook on her. I've always wondered if she wasn't fighting for you when she took Davenport to court."

"Fighting for me?" Casey repeated, astonished.

His brilliant eyes held hers. "I don't think she cared two cents for the notoriety and publicity. I think she was trying to safeguard her child's heritage."

Casey stared at him, startled.

"If your grandmother regains consciousness, ask her. Ask people who remember your mother."

"I will. Thank you for telling me," she said, stunned.

One afternoon as she sat alone holding Alice's hand, she suddenly understood what Kalin had needed from her five years ago, and why he felt hurt when she hadn't given it.

He had needed her to listen while he talked about his father. The more scandals and failed investments he uncovered, the more he had needed her sympathy and understanding.

Just her presence would have been sufficient. But she had been busy thinking about cooking school, and whether she'd have enough money saved. She had lost the man she loved.

Casey shuddered with horror at her own blind stupidity. She had thought she loved Kalin, but she hadn't offered him a tenth of the compassion and love he had given her the past few days.

He would never take another chance on her. Why should he? So far as he could see, she hadn't changed a bit in five years. He'd said as much, and she knew he was right.

Casey put her head down on the bed and wept. Soon her mild bout of tears turned into deep, wrenching sobs. No wonder Kalin had spurned her when she had begged him to come back to her. He'd probably known then that she wasn't going to change.

"You're utterly worn out," Bonnie told her that afternoon after one glance at her face. "What you need to do is go home and lie down. Everything looks better after a good night's sleep."

Casey agreed and wondered just how awful she looked.

"I'm going to stay all night," Bonnie said. "Poor Dr. Johnson was just telling me how worried is about you."

"I'm never sick." Casey studied Alice. The old woman lay much as she had for the past few days, unmoving unless the nurses turned her. "Thanks, Bonnie. I'll go home and rest a while."

The cell phone Kalin had given her chimed, and she took it from her pocket, reminded yet again of his care for her. "Yes, I'm fine, Kalin. Bonnie's here, and I'm going home to rest."

Bonnie tactfully went outside the room to give her privacy.

"I'll be tied up with a client and won't be able to get there until later tonight," he said.

"Kalin, I need to tell you something."

"Later, darling. Go home and to bed."

"You were right. I was trying to prove I wasn't like my mother. I deserved everything you said to me five years ago. I'm sorry it took me this long to realize it."

"If you start crying, I'll come over there and beat you." Kalin sounded alarmed. "What's caused this?"

Casey got a grip on herself. "I just wanted to tell you now, while it was on my mind." As if it wouldn't be on her mind for quite some time to come, she thought, with wry humor.

"Go to bed, Casey. Now. I'll be over later tonight."

"You don't have to come tonight. It's too long a drive."

"Of course I'm coming," he said. "Now go home to bed. I want to see you looking refreshed when I get there."

Casey went home, shooed on her way by Bonnie, and soon found herself wandering around the house like a lost spirit. She assessed the kitchen table, loaded with food offerings. The refrigerator was full to bursting. She wouldn't have to cook for a month. The freezer overflowed with fish, ducks, shrimp, and squirrels. The people she had baked for over the years had returned the favor in full.

She wandered into the living room and stared at the Christmas tree she sat gazing at every night. She had one unopened gift left, which meant—she checked her watch and smiled at the rising moon on the face—tonight was Old Christmas Eve. Still smiling, she glanced at the gifts Kalin had given her, most of them designed to convince her that fishing was good for the body and the soul.

The last two presents had been cooking gear, a heart-shaped tart pan and a set of heart-shaped cookie cutters. Perhaps she'd use them to bake something for him.

The final gift was a square box that had been professionally wrapped. Unlike the others, it had an envelope attached. She opened it, extracted the card it contained, and read: "Merry Old Christmas, Darling, From Someone Who Loves You."

She caught her breath and ripped off the green foil wrap and opened the box inside. She lifted out a framed, professionally done photograph of a young, blond woman, scarcely more than a child, whose fragile bone structure was Casey's own.

Casey sat back, balancing the photograph on her knees. The woman's eyes were large and blue and gazed upon the world with an innocent vulnerability that made one long to protect her. Her blond hair was straight and thick, and her mouth was Casey's, wide and generous.

Casey had never seen the photograph before, and she wondered where Kalin had found it.

He had been right, she realized. The child-woman in the picture was a woman who could easily become a victim of circumstances and her own heart. The notoriety-seeking tramp Casey had tried for years to live down had never existed.

For the second time that day, Casey cried, this time for the time she'd wasted feeling ashamed of someone who had, as Kalin pointed out, loved her and fought for her.

Propping the photograph beneath the tree, Casey got to her feet. She wandered into her bedroom, noting that the pale, winter sun was setting. Then she remembered it was Old Christmas Eve.

She carried her pillow and two quilts out to the barn. There, she built up a pile of hay and spread one quilt on it, and used the other as a blanket.

The sky rapidly darkened as she quickly opened the door to the chicken coop and carried the big red rooster and one of his hens, both protesting vigorously, to the rear of the old barn, perching them carefully on the edge of a stall. Then she shut the big, sliding door and felt her way in the failing light from the skylight directly overhead back to her quilts.

Young John Broussard had already put Cork, her grandfather's old plow horse, and Eloise, the milk cow, into their respective stalls. Both animals commented softly on Casey's presence, and with more vehemence on the loud bock-bock noises the chickens made. The animals sounded exactly like they had the night she and Kalin had spent together on a similar bed. The couple's passionate murmurs had kept the animals disturbed.

Within moments of curling up atop the pile of hay and snuggling one of the quilts up around her ears, the restlessness suddenly left her, and Casey fell soundly asleep.

She awakened some hours later to a dense blackness when a rooster's crow shattered the silence. Shuffling sounds and a nicker told her Cork and Eloise remained awake and unaccustomed to chickens inside the barn.

She might have slept one hour or six. She peered into the total, cold blackness and tried to orient herself before becoming aware of other presences in the old barn.

Dawn must have arrived, because she suddenly found she could see quite clearly what was near her, even though the far areas of the barn were still midnight black.

A woman approached her makeshift bed and smiled down on her.

"I figured you'd be out here, Casey," she said. "You should be ashamed of yourself. You fell asleep again."

"Why, Granny," Casey exclaimed. "You're well. Dr. Johnson said you weren't likely to recover."

"Jack Johnson is a smart man, but he doesn't know everything." Alice sat beside Casey on the hay.

Casey sat up and looked closely at her grandmother. Alice looked younger than Casey could recall ever seeing her.

"Why didn't you call me?" she asked. "I'd have come to the hospital and picked you up. Who brought you home?"

"Don't be silly," Alice said. "I don't need a car where I'm going."

"Can't you spend at least one night in your own bed before you take off? What time is it? I'll cook you some supper."

"Do you hear that, Ewing?" Alice turned to the man who approached down the long, central corridor of the barn, seeming to materialize out of the darkness. "She wants to cook for us."

"Grandpa," Casey exclaimed, unable to recall at the moment why she was surprised to see him. "Where have you been?"

"I've been on the other side of the universe." Ewing Gray laughed and came to stand beside Alice. "I came to apologize for accusing you of being pregnant."

"Sir?" Casey shivered in the cold barn air.

Ewing Gray smiled. "I knew you spent the night out here with that McBryde boy on Old Christmas Eve. Came out to check on you and heard voices. Sure enough, there was that red car of his parked on the dirt road behind the barn."

Casey thought a moment. "So you knew about that." Her brain refused to function. "Why didn't you come in and run him off?"

"It was four a.m.," Ewing said in dry tones. "I figured it was already too late. I didn't want to cause you to run away like your mother did. I accused you falsely and you ran anyway."

Casey shook her head. "I didn't leave because of you. I left because it was time. We didn't make love that night, you know."

"I know that," Ewing said. "Now."

"Kalin is trying to restore my self-esteem. Once he succeeds, he'll probably find a woman more worthy of him."

Ewing and Alice exchanged glances.

"That's the silliest thing I've ever heard you say," Alice said. "What makes you think you aren't worthy of him?"

Casey balanced her chin on her knees. "He's been so good to me, and I've failed him miserably."

Ewing Gray sat down on the hay bed beside Alice, and Casey obligingly scooted over to make room. The white shock of hair falling across his forehead that Casey had thought so handsome when she was a child looked darker. No doubt it was a trick of the strange half-light in the barn.

"It seems to me that you have a little problem, Casey," Ewing said. "You've hurt him, and now you're unwilling to go to him and ask his forgiveness."

"I'm not unwilling," Casey said. "But some things are difficult to overcome in a single apology. He has a right to know I've changed, and that takes time to prove. By then he might be married to Sunny Cansler or somebody like her."

"Who's Sunny Cansler?" Ewing asked.

"The Houston Canslers are definite social improvements over an unknown country bastard," a new voice struck in.

"Who are you?" Casey grabbed for a weapon and came up with only a handful of hay. "What are you doing here?"

Walter McBryde looked at her contemptuously. Casey had never met him, but she recognized the lean, chiseled face and broad, slashing eyebrows instantly.

"The door was open." He laughed coldly. "You never will be worthy of my son. He will be a great man someday."

Alice and Ewing Gray looked at him with pity.

"It was Jack Johnson who raised that boy and saw that he turned into a decent human being," Alice said. "You'd have ruined him. *If* you had ever paid him any attention."

Walter McBryde seemed to swell in his exquisitely tailored

business suit. "Jack Johnson will never be anything more than an unknown country doctor."

"And a darned fine one," Ewing Gray said. "Plus, he's already got what people like you slave all their lives to get—a place in the country with plenty of hunting and fishing nearby."

Behind her, someone laughed outright. Casey turned and saw a slim, shapely woman, with great blue eyes and thick golden hair. The blond wore a short skirt that exposed a pair of eye-stopping, long legs.

"Sic 'em, Daddy," the blond said.

"Not one word more out of you, young lady," Ewing Gray said.

Casey admired the blond's fine-boned figure and delicately sculpted face, wondering how she had gotten into the barn. There must be another entrance she had temporarily forgotten, because a man had joined the blond, a man whose darkly handsome face and expressive gray eyes had captivated a generation of women.

"You're a loser," Derrick Davenport told Walter McBryde. "Not even your own son respects your memory." He gave his famous movie star chuckle. "Join the club, old boy."

"What do you know about it?" Walter McBryde sneered. "You're no better. For a man who repudiated his daughter and legally evaded child support payments so he could marry that whore, Megan Murphy, you sound like a preacher."

Derrick smiled at Casey. "Actually, my daughter is better off. What do you think her life would have been like if every reporter knew who she was and where she was? I did my child a favor, old boy. But that's neither here nor there."

"Right," Alice said. "Both of you stay out of this. I've got something I've been wanting to say to Casey for some time. I should have spoken sooner." She turned to Casey, who was staring, bemused, at Derrick Davenport and the slender blond at his side. "Now pay attention, Casey Gray. Your young man was right. Using your mother's tragedy as a threat to make you behave was very wrong of me."

Casey transferred her gaze to her grandmother and wondered why she felt she had strayed into a madhouse.

"I didn't realize the impression you'd gain from it," Alice said. "It simply never occurred to me that you'd think she was a money-hungry tart who preferred to earn her living on her back."

Casey swallowed and looked down, ashamed.

"She wasn't like that at all," Alice said. "She was a dreamer, and she had that same steadfast determination to achieve her goals that you have. If you'd ever asked, I could have told you about her. I should have overcome my hurt and told you anyway, but thinking about Cynthia and the way we failed her always made me cry."

Alice nodded briskly as Casey's eyes widened in comprehension. She added, "Remember how I told you Ewing and I were terrified when I came home with you in my arms? It was as if we had a second chance, and we'd better not muff it this time."

Casey stared at her up-drawn knees. Over the past week she had begun to understand why her grandparents had been so grimly determined to rear her carefully.

"So in a way, it was our fault you lost your young man. But it's your fault if you don't do anything to get him back," Alice finished.

"Oh, don't be so hard on her, Mom," the blond said. "You're the one who made her think she had to work like a slave so she wouldn't turn out like me. No wonder the poor kid was so messed up. Casey, honey, the last thing that young man wants is for you to be ashamed of the way he makes you feel. Heck, he's even willing to beg for your favors if that's what it takes."

Casey stared at the blond.

"No, I don't feel ashamed of begging Derrick to marry me. I loved him, you know, and I wanted my baby to have her father. Besides, I might have succeeded. You have to take risks on people. You win some—"

"Hold your tongue, Cynthia," Alice said.

"Why should I?" the blond asked. "It's high time I got to have my say. Casey, baby, you go out there and seduce old Walter's son. He's already crazy about you, and there's nothing like a romp in the bedroom to clear things up."

Alice snorted. "Is that your philosophy?"

Cynthia laughed. "Come on, Mom. I knew where I stood with Derrick all along. I just didn't want to believe it."

Casey blinked and shook her head. "Now I know what's wrong here. This is a dream. All of you except Granny are dead. I knew there was something weird about this."

Cynthia tilted one hip forward in imitation of a model's stance. "You're the one who believes in all Mom's nonsense about Old Christmas. And they do say spirits walk on Old Christmas Eve."

"I'm getting out of here." Casey felt her hair attempting to lift off her scalp. "Come on, Granny."

Alice chuckled. "No one here means you any harm, Casey. We all want the same thing—your happiness."

Casey reached out tentatively to touch Alice. Alice's skin was warm and solid, not cool and fragile as it had been in the hospital.

Casey swallowed and regarded her grandmother in shock.

Alice smiled. "Don't try to hold me, Casey. I'm more than ready to go. It's Old Christmas Eve, you know. I only came to apologize for teaching you to be ashamed of your mother's actions. I simply didn't realize how it would affect you."

Casey squeezed her eyes shut, then opened them again, and forked her hair back to stare wildly around the barn. She couldn't see two inches in front of her face.

She was alone.

Chapter 12

"Casey? Are you in here?"

Kalin's voice cut through the dense blackness, and she heard the scraping sounds as he pushed the heavy, sliding door aside.

The animals commented in various ways on the disturbance.

"Toward the back." Casey realized she trembled like one of her most tender custards.

"Thank God."

She heard the door scrape shut, then a small beam of light bounced over the walls and played down the long, central corridor. Footsteps approached, and moments later, the beam located her makeshift bed.

"I got worried when no one answered the door, so I found the key and went in. Why didn't you leave me a note or carry your phone with you?" Kalin sat down beside her on the hay.

Casey noted absently that the bed had shifted in exactly the same way when Ewing Gray had sat down beside her. Once more, the hair gently lifted off her scalp.

"I'm sorry. I didn't think of a note." She reached beneath the quilt and produced the phone. "And I do have my phone." She sounded strangled. "But it never rang."

"You nearly gave me a heart attack," he said. "Your bed hadn't been touched, but you'd opened your present. Then I remembered it was Old Christmas Eve."

She felt his fingers touch her cheek, then his lips found hers. Casey flung her arms around him, trembling, and wished she could melt her body into his.

"Are you cold, darling?" He ran his hands lightly over her sweatshirt. "You're shivering. Let's go back to the house."

Casey drew in a deep breath. "I'm all right. I'd rather stay here for a little longer. It reminds me of old times."

He laid her back on the quilt and stretched out beside her. "I hope your memories are as good as mine."

"Better, probably. Kalin, I have something to tell you."

"Don't say anything, darling. Kiss me."

Casey kissed him with all the passion at her command, and sighed with pleasure when he ran his fingers into her hair and held her face still while he kissed her eyelids and her nose. He hadn't shaved and his chin scraped the delicate skin of her face, but Casey loved it.

The time had come to take a chance. She had no idea where the thought had come from, but she agreed with it wholeheartedly.

You win some . . .

"Kalin, I love you," she said quickly. "Will you marry me?"

"Yes," he said immediately. He came up on his elbow to lean over her, even though he couldn't see her face. "Provided the wedding is very soon. Say, within the next two weeks."

His lack of hesitation gratified her. "How about next week?"

"You have yourself a deal." He laughed, a breathless, happy sound in the darkness. "Once I'm your husband, I can put my foot down and make you stay in bed for a week."

"I'll stay there now, if you stay with me."

"I'm afraid to ask what brought this on," he said. "So I'm not going to."

She forestalled him by locking her arms around his neck and pulling his face down to hers. She knew at once when he relaxed and began concentrating on what he felt.

Automatically, her mouth opened to allow his entry, and he followed up the small surrender by demanding more and more. By the time he broke the kiss, they both needed air.

"Let's go to the house." Kalin nuzzled her neck. "It's Old Christmas Eve, you know. We don't want your grandfather's spirit searching for his shotgun."

Casey choked with laughter. "He knew we were together out here that time on Old Christmas Eve. That's why he thought for sure I was pregnant."

"He knew? I'm lucky he didn't shoot me. He'd never have believed we didn't make love. Stop that," he said with a groan. "We're disturbing your rooster."

Casey threaded her fingers into his hair. "My mother said there's nothing like a romp in the bedroom to clarify things."

She used her hold in his hair to lock his lips to hers while she teased him mercilessly with her tongue. Kalin returned the caress, allowing his body to seek hers once more.

Casey rested her hands on his shoulders. "I love you, Kalin. I want to have your babies, and cook delicious things for you. I'll even defeather your ducks, and clean your fish." She paused and added, "Every now and then."

"What happened out here tonight?" he asked. "Don't tell me. I probably don't want to know. Next, you'll be inviting me on a fishing trip."

"How about this weekend?" she interposed quickly.

"Oh, Lord." His chest was moving with his laughter. "You act like a person who's seen the ghosts of Christmas Past, Present, and Future. How long will this conversion last?"

"Until the birth of our first child, which will probably be within nine months of the wedding. At that time, I'll have to give up the fishing trips for a while."

Kalin buried his face against her neck, still chuckling. "I almost forgot. I have some interesting news for you, darling."

"What is it?"

"You're going to have to postpone your plans for instant pregnancy."

Casey stiffened. "What for? I thought we discussed this five years ago. Have you changed your mind?"

Kalin never stopped laughing. That in itself aroused her mistrust. She wound her fingers into his crisp hair and tugged.

"All right, Kalin McBryde. What have you done?"

"*Me*? I'm innocent. It's just that nursing a baby while you're attending law school would be a major stress on you."

"You know good and well I never had any intention of going to law school. Besides, I've probably flunked the LSAT." She tugged harder on his hair. "Stop laughing."

"Sorry. It's a bit difficult. Especially when I was contacted today by the SETEX Farmers Auxiliary. They've established a scholarship fund at the Gulf Coast Bank. They want to help pay your way to law school."

Casey froze, horrified. The SETEX Farmers Auxiliary was a group of older women whose husbands had been involved in rice farming. Alice had belonged, and Casey had spent many a night baking special items for members who had lost a loved one.

"Oh, no," she whispered.

"They thought I would know how to set up the account and oversee the—the scholarship fund," Kalin said and dissolved once more into laughter.

"This is not funny, Kalin." Casey sat up, alarmed. "You didn't set it up, did you? How could you? And they've gone so far as to collect money? Oh, this is awful."

"It's only a small postponement of your plans," Kalin pointed out. "After you've completed law school, we can get started on the four children. Now, Casey, be reasonable. After the ladies have gone through this much trouble—stop that."

Casey attacked him, rolled him over on the quilt and almost tumbled him off the haystack.

"I've got a plan," she announced.

"I'm not sure I want to hear it. Especially if it involves telling those nice old ladies—what are you doing?"

Casey straddled him and trapped his face between her palms, kissed him once more and unbuttoned the top button of his shirt.

"We're going to get a head start on the children," she said. "If

I'm safely pregnant by the time the LSAT scores come out, the ladies will be understanding when I suggest that they donate the scholarship to another deserving local individual."

"Something tells me you're aiming to get me plugged full of ghostly buckshot."

"Don't you want to cooperate in saving me from law school? What if I do better than you did?"

"I'd be damned glad. Then I could stay home and write while you put up with all the crap young lawyers have to put up with from the older lawyers, the peculiar rulings of judges, and the crazy clients. Not to mention the mean clients, the vengeful clients, and the spaced-out clients."

"I am so *not* going to law school," she insisted. "That's my final word on the subject. How you get me out of it is your affair."

"If you passed the LSAT, you probably owe it to the world to become a lawyer. Especially if you really aced it."

"You're enjoying this, Kalin McBryde."

"You'd better believe it. I'm going to love having a smart wife who can support me in style. If you don't go to law school, you'll have to buy Cap'n Bob's and turn it into a big sensation. We need a regular income if I'm going to maintain the positive mental attitude that will allow me to write my three or four novels a year."

"You can't do this to me," she wailed. "It's evil."

"On your feet, you shameless hussy. When you start messing around with my future income, it's time to postpone the lovemaking and attend to the subject of income generation. I'll call Joe—"

Casey rolled him over once more and lay on top of him, kissing him while she fitted her hips against his. After a minute or two of that, Kalin lost interest in sending her to law school and set about showing her how best to please him. She devoted herself to the subject, secure in the knowledge that he would please her just as thoroughly.

Later, as they curled together beneath the quilt, Kalin said softly, "I stopped by the hospital before I came looking for you. Your grandmother is doing as well as can be expected, according to Uncle Jack."

Casey realized abruptly that Alice no longer inhabited the comatose body that lay so still in the hospital.

Kalin hugged her and said tenderly, "We can wait to be married until after things settle down."

"I've already gotten the word from her." Casey snuggled her face against his neck. "The sooner I marry you, the sooner she can quit worrying about my future, or what that cooking school has done to me."

"Is that right?" Kalin grinned. "In that case, I'll get things set up right away. Do you want a church wedding, or will a justice of the peace do?"

"Granny would have a fit, but I'd rather the JP."

"If she gets better, we can be remarried in the church."

Casey nodded, touching one of his broad eyebrows.

"Darling, don't cry."

Casey put her face against his shoulder. "I never even asked if you'd forgiven me. I'm so sorry, Kalin. It wasn't until today that I suddenly understood why you broke up with me five years ago. I was going to promise to change before I asked you to marry me."

"Darling, once we're married, you're going to have to change." He held her, kissing her forehead. "If you think I'll let you rattle pots and pans in the kitchen while I'm waiting for you in bed, forget it."

"You should at least make me swear on the Bible, or sign something in blood. It's the minimum I deserve after being so selfish."

"You weren't selfish, Casey," he said gently. "You were just very single-minded. Once I started checking into your background, I began to understand how your history and upbringing had affected you. Imagine how I felt when I realized how badly the things I'd said had hurt you."

"They didn't hurt me as much as I deserved." Casey lifted her face but could see nothing in the darkness. "You were right about one thing. I should have reminded you of how you responded when we kissed. You were as enthusiastic about it as I was."

"Maybe more. I hoped to win you back by showing you gradually that certain things between us hadn't changed."

"I hope they never do," Casey said, and kissed him.

At dawn, they returned to the house at last, and Casey looked around the kitchen. The old farmhouse looked the same as it had the evening before, yet everything had changed somehow. Perhaps the inanimate objects sensed that their mistress had departed. Or perhaps she saw things from an entirely different perspective.

She blinked back tears and glanced up to see Kalin's concerned, blue gaze on her face. "You look different, darling," he said. "More at peace."

She stepped into his arms. "I never realized it before, but I was terribly driven, and for all the reasons you said. Thank you, Kalin."

Kalin's arms tightened around her. "Thank me? For what? For hurting your feelings so badly you had to stay away for five years?"

"For caring enough about me to point it out. I don't know if I would have ever stopped to reason it out on my own. It was easier to work until I was too tired to think."

"That was what terrified me." He kissed her ear. "I was afraid you'd collapse before I could get through to you. If your grandfather was still alive, he would probably have shot me for sure."

Casey refused to let him move out of her arms. "Actually, he and Granny are very pleased that I've finally come to my senses, and that the old homestead is going to be the home of a new generation of Gray descendants."

Kalin chuckled. "Did I ever tell you your grandfather took me aside one day and mentioned, perfectly casually, exactly what he'd do to me if I was so rash as to take advantage of your underage, feminine loveliness?"

"Grandpa said that?"

"He did, I promise you. He sounded remarkably like Uncle Jack."

"Grandpa?" Casey was shaking her head.

"He was remembering your mother, darling. From all I can find out, every young stud at East Chambers High was panting after her."

Casey hugged him, hard. "That's another thing. You gave me back my mother."

"Hush, darling." He kissed her eyelids. "I just talked to people who remembered her. The more I heard, the more I began to realize that there was another explanation for her behavior. You had a right to know that."

"Thank you." She drew in a quivering breath. "You can't imagine what it meant to me to know that she fought for me."

Kalin sifted his fingers through her hair. "You were definitely worth fighting for, darling. In this case, I'm glad she didn't succeed. Your life would have been totally different if you had been recognized as Derrick Davenport's daughter."

"That's what he said." Casey closed her eyes and enjoyed the feel of Kalin's fingers. "He claims he did me a favor."

"Is that so?"

She opened her eyes and saw Kalin smiling at her.

"Do you want to know what else my mother said?"

"Of course." His smile widened.

"She said I should seduce you, because the last thing you wanted was for me to be ashamed of the way you made me feel."

Kalin nodded. "I was ready to throw away all the promises I'd made myself and take advantage of your physical response to me. Then I was going to insist that you quit work and marry me, especially if you got pregnant. At the time, it looked as though that was the only way."

She grinned. "So why didn't you?"

"You saved me the trouble." He led her to the living room. "What happened out there tonight?"

"Didn't I tell you that spirits walk on Old Christmas Eve?"

Kalin glanced cautiously around the room. "Did I ever tell you I was the sort of easily terrorized kid who stayed awake nights for months after telling ghost stories around a campfire?"

"No, and if you did, I wouldn't believe you."

"If you're going to tell me you talked to your mother's spirit tonight, I don't think I want to hear it." He glanced around once more, then gave in to curiosity. "Did you see anyone else?"

"They were all here. Your father, my father—"

"*My* father?"

"He doesn't think I'm good enough for you."

"That sounds about like him," Kalin said, disgusted.

"My father told him his own son doesn't respect his memory. Maybe you ought to respect your dad's memory a little more. I'd rather not have him infesting my visions next year."

Kalin stared at her, clearly uneasy.

"Granny apologized for teaching me to be ashamed of my mother's history. As you said, she didn't realize the impression I'd get. Grandpa came, and so did my mother."

Kalin let his breath out on a long sigh. "It sounds like they were all eager to talk."

"Granny said all they wanted was my happiness." She grimaced, disappointed. "Do you think this means they won't be coming to see me next Old Christmas Eve?"

"Once you're married and happy?" Kalin laughed. "Talk about an incentive to keep you happy." He bent to pick up a small package that had been newly placed beneath the Christmas tree and handed it to her. "It's now officially Old Christmas day, so you can open the last package now."

She took the beautifully wrapped little box and worked at the wrapping while Kalin pulled her down to sit beside him on the sofa.

"Here. Let me do it." Impatient, he took the box and shucked off the wrapper. "I want to see you wearing that." He extracted a glittering diamond ring and slid it on her left hand.

"Oh, Kalin, it's beautiful." Casey's surprise gave way to great joy as she realized Kalin had intended to ask her to marry him before she proposed to him. "I wish Granny could see it." Her smile went crooked. "She told me not to let you give me a diamond ring, or the stone would end up in someone's breakfast biscuit."

He laughed. "Then we'll get you another one. Don't you know I'd give you anything you want?"

"That's supposed to be my line." She stared at the Christmas tree he had given her and dropped her gaze to the photograph of her mother. "You've already given me so much."

"Actually, you've given me even more." He touched her lips tenderly with his index finger. "And that's not even mentioning that you've done more for my sister than all the expensive counselors Mom took her to. So don't be surprised if Mom tries to give you a car for a wedding gift."

"Lydia?"

"My dad," Kalin said. "He had started drinking more and more, and then he'd come home and start in on Mom and Lydia. They didn't want to worry me, so I never knew a thing about it until after he died. Lydia was a basket case for a while there."

Casey closed her eyes, thinking of Lydia's bright beauty. "Lydia has a real vocation in the restaurant business. All she needed was a good restaurant to test her skills on."

"You've made me happy, my mother happy, and you've made my sister happy," he enumerated. "What can I do to make you happy, darling?"

"Do you really want to know?"

He looked at her with some alarm. "What?"

She smiled and fluttered her eyelashes at him. "Get the SETEX Farmer's Auxiliary to award that law school scholarship to someone else."

"That will not be easy." Kalin regarded the Christmas tree in thoughtful silence.

"I know, but if anyone can manage it, it's you."

He turned to her and took her in his arms. "In return, I want a promise from you that I never have to spend another Old Christmas Eve in the barn. If I see my Dad, or even yours, I can guarantee you I'll never be the same."

Casey promised and kissed him with all the love in her heart. Somehow she held in her laughter, although the effort required was enormous.

"What?" he asked, when he was able to speak.

"Someday your little girl will want to spend the night in the barn, and you'll have to — "

"Bite your tongue."

"As for the Ladies Auxiliary, I still think the best plan is to have a baby right away."

"They created that scholarship especially for you." He looked thoughtfully at the Christmas tree again. "I hate to disappoint them."

"Do you have any better ideas?"

"Yes. I'm going to make love to you again."

Casey blinked, then laughed shakily.

"So long as you have a concrete plan of action," she said, and slipped her arms around his neck.

Recipe

Deep Dark Secret Cheesecake Cookie Crust

Ingredients:

3 cups dark chocolate wafers, finely crumbled

¼ lb. unsalted butter, melted

Instructions:

1. Mix crumbs with melted butter and stir well.
2. Press into chilled, buttered 10-inch springform pan.
3. Bake in preheated 350-degree F oven for 10 minutes.
4. Cool, then chill in refrigerator.

Cheesecake Filling

Ingredients:

Twelve 1-ounce pieces semisweet chocolate

3 tablespoons unsalted butter

Five 8-ounce packages cream cheese

1 cup sugar

1 tablespoon vanilla

6 large eggs

2 egg yolks

1 cup heavy cream

3 tablespoons unsweetened cocoa powder

Crust

Instructions:

1. Prepare cheesecake casing.

2. Bring all ingredients to room temperature by allowing them to set out of the refrigerator for at least 2 hours.

3. Combine the semisweet chocolate pieces and the butter in a double boiler and melt. Set aside to cool to room temperature.

4. Beat the cream cheese at medium speed with an electric mixer until it is smooth. Do not overbeat.

5. Add sugar in thirds, blending well at medium speed after each addition.

6. Add vanilla.

7. In a separate bowl, combine all eggs and egg yolks and beat lightly. Add beaten eggs, a third at a time, to creamed mixture, beating lightly to incorporate the eggs throughout the mixture.

8. Add cooled melted chocolate and heavy cream in thirds, alternating chocolate and cream and beating at medium speed after each addition.

9. Sift the cocoa powder over the cheese mixture in thirds, beating at medium speed after each addition.

10. Using a rubber spatula, stir the sides of the mixture down, then begin folding the mixture, going deep into the bowl and over the top, for 3 to 5 minutes.

11. Gently fold mixture into prepared casing or crust.

12. Bake in preheated 350-degree F oven for 15 minutes. Reduce oven temperature to 275 degrees and bake for 50 minutes for a soft-set center. For a firm-set center, bake for 1 hour.

13. Crack the oven door slightly, using a wooden spoon wedged in the top of the door to hold it open slightly, and cool in this manner for 1 hour.

14. Take a very thin, short spatula, open the oven door, and working swiftly, without jiggling the cheesecake, ream around the metal ring of the springform pan twice to loosen the cheesecake from the edge of the pan.

15. Close the oven door, leaving the wooden spoon to hold it slightly ajar, and allow the cheesecake to cool completely in the oven for 6 to 8 hours then refrigerate.

About The Author

Kathryn Brocato was born in Texas, grew up in Arkansas and graduated from high school and college in Southeast Texas, where she and her husband, Charles, are scientists and business owners. A true believer in the happy ending, she is a lifelong reader and writer of romance. When she is not writing, Kathryn enjoys birding, gardening, and tending her backyard chicken flock.

In the mood for more Crimson Romance? Check out *Catch of the Year* by Brenda Hammond at *CrimsonRomance.com*.

Printed in the United States
By Bookmasters